WEIRD

URBAN FANTASY WALKS

DIGBETH, BIRMINGHAM

Edited by
ADRIAN MIDDLETON

For those writers of Almanacks, Compendia and Miscellanies
who placed history in our hands.

First published in Great Britain' in 2013 by
FRINGEWORKS LTD
IN ASSOCIATION WITH BEORMA CARE CIC AND THE
DIGBETH TRUST

Weird Trails 2

CONTENTS

INTRODUCTION

View of Birmingham from old Cheapside, William Hutton's *An History of Birmingham.*

Birmingham has always had a great literary heritage, particularly in relation to areas of 'genre' fiction, science fiction, fantasy and horror, perhaps this is due to spreading of the industrial landscape, radiating outwards from the town centre like a dark stain that threatened to become a blight on the English countryside. That certainly inspired Tolkien's works, as a reaction against man's crimes against nature, and it was certainly a factor in the birth of heavy metal.

The writings of Washington Irving were inspired by his numerous visits to stay with friends in Birmingham, from 1815 onwards.

Birmingham-born Jane Louden's *The Mummy* (1827), a direct reaction to Mary Shelley's *Frankenstein*, was one of the earliest instances of science fiction to appear in Britain, while Bromsgrove-born Clemence Housman's *The Were-wolf* (1896) perhaps dissuaded Bram Stoker from including a similar creature in his final draft of *Dracula*; and of course, much of J.R.R. Tolkien's Middle-Earth is based upon his boyhood experiences in and around Birmingham.

Grant Allen, W. H. Auden, Rev. Wilbert Awdry, Dame Barbara Cartland, Lee Child, Sir Arthur Conan Doyle, Lindsey Davis, John Hampson, Roi Kwabena, Louis Macneice, John Meaney, Sadie Plant, Sax Rohmer, John Wyndham, the list of those who came from, or spent a significant amount of time in, Birmingham, goes on and on. The city is also home to the *Birmingham Science Fiction Group*, the UK's longest running SF fanclub.

With such a colourful heritage behind it, I therefore found myself somewhat appalled when, while attending *Eastercon 2013*, an urban fantasy panel (made up of authors who had all written London-based urban fantasy novels) replied to the question "why are all urban fantasies set in London?" with "well, who'd want to set one in Birmingham?"

Being a loyal Brummie, I had to respond. While London has a rich and well-documented history supported by layer-upon-layer of archaeological evidence, Birmingham is quite the opposite. Its origins as an early Anglo-Saxon settlement remain speculative, as does the identity of its founder, and there are scant records of its early centuries until the medieval market town emerged from the shadow of neighbouring Coventry.

While Birmingham's political pedigree is as fine as that of any city, even its sons and daughters think back only as far as the Industrial Revolution, when the town's growth spurted to such a degree it was briefly the fastest-growing town in Europe, or to the Birmingham Blitz, when the city, along with Coventry to the east, was targeted for destruction by the Luftwaffe.

But these are the very reasons why Birmingham is the perfect setting for modern urban fantasy. The mystery of its role within the ancient border kingdom of Mercia, whose written record seems to have been erased by its enemies and successors, is ripe for creative exploitation. The many and rapid layers of archaeology laid down in a short space of time as the town was transformed, shifting from farmers markets to parliamentarian forge-masters, chain-makers and navvies, bankers and manufacturers, car makers and bomb victims. The very reinvention of Birmingham as an industrial city has perhaps wiped away more culture and heritage than any other city would allow, leaving a tragic scar swallowed up by its adoption of new cultures and customs, making it the largest and most culturally diverse British city outside of London itself.

Weird Trails is therefore an attempt to redress an awful slight, to set a benchmark for the other towns and cities beyond London, and finally to tell stories that might inspire writers looking for new and different settings. Urban fantasy has a home in Birmingham and in those other places, and these books will set down the marker for others to follow, bringing together a walking trail and guide with some of the best urban fantasy that the boys and girls of *old Brummagem* can muster.

ADRIAN MIDDLETON, SEPTEMBER 2013

THE CITY OF A THOUSAND NAMES

Full twenty years and more have passed since I left Brumagem,
But I set out for home at last, to good old Brumagem.
But every place is altered so, there›s hardly a single place I know
Which fills my heart with grief and woe, I can't find Brumagem.

- Dobbs, a comedian

Actually, Birmingham only has around a hundred and forty six variant names, mostly the result of a large working population that came and went from the town, spreading its reputation by word of mouth. What is was known as, 'was the city of a thousand trades', built up from back-street forges and knock-off shops that once made the term 'Made in Birmingham' as recognisable as 'Made in China' or 'Made in Taiwan' is today.

Birmingham is more and more becoming a 'found city', its lost secrets slowly unlocked by progressive archaeology. For although it has only been a city since 1889, its origins stretch back to before the founding of many more obviously Anglo-Saxon settlements, and it has many as-yet-uncharted layers that exist because, for some reason, Birmingham is a city that never stands still long enough for the historians to properly take stock.

Digbeth lies at the heart of this archaeological voyage of discovery, with major reinventions in the twelfth, thirteenth, sixteenth, seventeenth, eighteenth, nineteenth, twentieth and twenty-first centuries; and since the Industrial Revolution, Birmingham has been the fastest growing and largest settlement outside of the city of London. So large and fast has this development been, that its satellites feared its spread. Local townships still fear and resent the spread of Birmingham today, while those on the outskirts of the region already see towns like Sandwell, Dudley, Solihull, Sutton and Walsall as its suburbs, and this in turn fuels fears that the West Midlands conurbation will spread even further.

Like many old towns, Birmingham featured in stories about prehistoric giants, whose interactions have become a metaphor for relationships between the boroughs. These historic rivalries have, it can be argued, led to measures being put in place, time and again, to curb Birmingham's growth. The Queensway, or the concrete collar, around the city centre, for example; the Outer Ring Road that separates the city from its suburbs; the green belts, like Sandwell Valley to the west and Sutton Park to the east. All have stalled Birmingham's inevitable expansion, which continues to this day. Birmingham still has the largest immigrant population in Britain, and was set to be the first city where the population was mostly non-white, a situation not changed by internal forces, but by a boost in Eastern European migrants who, like those that came before, changed the landscape of the city they now call home.

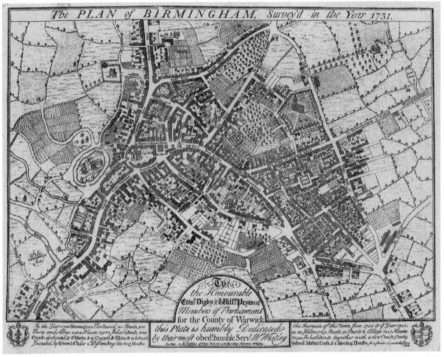

William Westley's Map of Birmingham, 1731

So what is Birmingham, and how does Digbeth factor into its origins? The area was settled long before the Anglo-Saxon came. Mesolithic settlements have been found, along with evidence of Roman roads, forts and salt mines close by. Britons already occupied the fringes of the ancient Forest of Arden where the counties of Staffordshire, Warwickshire and Worcestershire converged, and these included settlements at Dudley, Yardley, Wednesbury and Walsall, all of which surrounded the boggy, gravelly forest clearing cut out by the Rivers Tame, Cole and Rea.

It is the Rea Valley that was settled by the Mierce, or Mercians, settlers from across the North Sea who dared to push their way inland, settling between and among the places where the British still lived. Making their way downriver from Tamworth, these foreigners followed the River Tame until, somewhere in the vicinity of Digbeth and Highgate, they found the Rea Valley, and embarked upon building one or more settlements in the patchy clearings adjacent to the waterlogged banks of the muddy river. They are said to have been called the *beormings*, the family of Beorma, after whom the city is supposed to have been founded. The evidence is slight, and even the name Beorma wasn't known to have been used until an etymologist called Eilert Ekwall pulled it from the ether during the mid-1950s. Indeed, Showell's *Dictionary of Birmingham*, published in 1885, put forward a very different proposal:

> *"in Canute's reign there was an Earl Beorn, the king's nephew, and it has been fancifully suggested that in this name Beorn may lie the much-sought root for the etymology of the town's name. Beorn, or Bern, being derived from ber, a bear or boar, it might be arranged thusly:—*
>
> *"Ber, bear or boar; moeng, many; ham, dwelling—the whole making Bermoengham, the dwelling of many bears, or the home of many pigs!"*

So, we don't even know if Beorma existed, let alone whether he settled with his tribe, or whether he named them long before their arrival. The names Beornmund, Berm, Birm and Brom have all been put forward as possible names for this mythic founder, but for the best part of sixty years Ekwall's naming has stuck, and now Beorma will pass into legend as the builder of the city.

Such uncertainty is the canvas upon which legends are written. Birmingham is well into its second century as a city, and from a historical perspective two hundred years is about the time that such legends become established. Just as Romulus and Remus retrospectively became the mythic founders of Rome, and Robin Hood became synonymous with Nottingham, so too is Beorma capable of becoming a legendary icon for Birmingham.

Digbeth, meanwhile, is recognised as the oldest Birmingham settlement, built to the south of the confluence of the Tame and the Rea, upon the line of an old road that passes between Coventry in the east and Wolverhampton in the west, a line that doubtless formed a path through old Arden. It also lies between two of the old Roman roads, Icknield Street and Watling Street, that passed through the area before it was settled.

As the high town grew up on the hill looking down upon the Rea Valley, so too did Digbeth, first with its pools and wells, then its mills, its tanneries and its forges. Cutting through the suburbs was the muddy Holloway along which the livestock would be brought in to the town's market. Always the focus of local industry, Digbeth is where the migrants came for work, where the slums rose and fell, where the pubs and the back-to-back housing replaced them, where the importers and the warehouses were built over old, flooded meadows, forcing the water-starved river down beneath the surface of the town which, with the rise of industry, became a city. With so much filth, and poverty, and transience, Digbeth became a hive of unruly behaviour where the local gangs congregated, and where the first whiff of reform started to take place, bringing free libraries, chapels of temperance and hostelries for the homeless workers to the growing city.

Digbeth is both the oldest and the newest part of the city, torn down and rebuilt so many times that often only the shapes of ancient plots remain, with only the remnants of Victoriana standing testament to the suburb's role in the growth of Birmingham. It is claimed by the local Irish community, by the more recent Polish community, and latterly by an emerging creative community. It is surely only a matter of time before the myths and legends of its many cultures make a mark on their adopted home.

THE DIGBETH WALK

A walk through any town or city is a walk through history, and just like any history, it is made up of layers – the geography, the architecture, the events, the people, they all come together to tell a vivid story about the life and times of those who came before.

To many, Digbeth is an old industrial backwater of little interest to any but a historian or a property developer, but to those who look closely enough, there's something else. Digbeth is a scarred patchwork of the old and the new, the neglected and the revered. It is a place where industries were born, where great businesses rose to prominence, but also where poor people suffered, where immigrants first laid down their roots on English soil, and where the dreams of rich innovators were made real by the soot-stained hands of cheap labour.

It is also full of hidden places. A magnet for artists and a vault for historic mysteries. There are shades of old London and even New York in Birmingham, and much of what we find there has echoes all over the world.

THE CUSTARD FACTORY, GIBB STREET

The Custard Factory complex, as seen from Floodgate Street

 Let us begin our journey at the heart of modern Digbeth, in Gibb Square, which forms a hub around which much of the area's activities now revolve. Here, beneath the Green Man's gaze, festivals and flea markets come and go, and the city's creative community has gathered and grown in recent times.

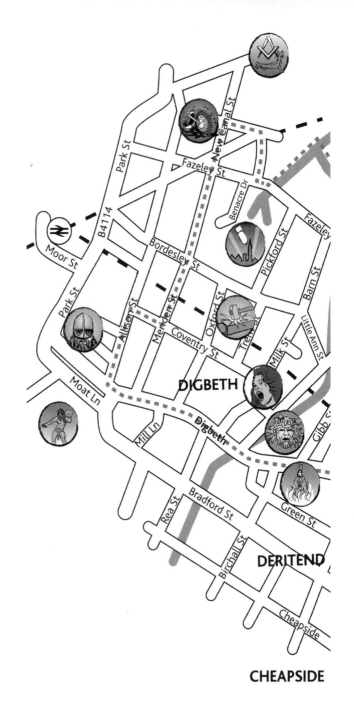

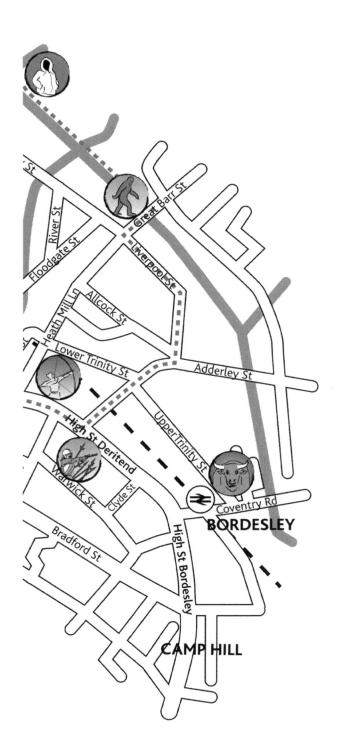

River St

Great Barr St

Floodgate St

Liverpool St

Heath Mill Ln

Allcock St

Lower Trinity St

Adderley St

High St Deritend

Upper Trinity St

Warwick St

Clyde St

Coventry Rd

BORDESLEY

Bradford St

High St Bordesley

CAMP HILL

The Custard Factory complex, from Lloyd's Bank to the Devonshire Works

BIRD'S CUSTARD

In 1902, *Alfred Bird & Sons* set to manufacturing their patented egg-free instant custard at the Devonshire Works Custard Factory in Digbeth. Alfred Bird had been a Birmingham chemist and druggist whose wife, Elizabeth, had an egg and yeast allergy. This led him, in 1843, to substitute egg with cornflour in the making of custard, and later to invent baking powder in order to make yeast-free bread.

Alfred Junior followed in his father's footsteps by inventing modern blancmange in 1867, egg-substitute in 1890, and jelly crystal powder in 1895. Under his guidance, *Bird's Custard* became a global brand that survives to this day, employing a workforce of a thousand.

The company moved to Banbury in 1964, and the premises fell into disuse until 1992 when, in the hands of entrepreneur Bennie Gray, who had previously redeveloped a water closet manufacturers in London's Mayfair. Better known as *Gray's Antique Centre*, his earlier venture is well known for having an exposed tributary of the River Tyburn in its basement; and so the idea of bringing new life to an old factory didn't faze him in the slightest, and with help from a mix of private investments and public funding, he poured millions into its redevelopment over the next twenty years. He started by hiring out space to a local theatre group, who made him aware of how desperate the creative industries were for business space, and his efforts to meet their needs has seen the site expand to cover an area of five acres, comprising the Custard Factory, Gibb Square (home to the Green Man), the Greenhouse, *Zellig* (formerly Devonshire House) and the Old Free Library. Bennie's son, Lucan, after making further investments to develop adjacent properties that include the former premises of *W.J.Wilde & Co* and a former Victorian chapel and Sunday school (now known as Fazeley Studios) took over the management of the complex in 2011.

Gibb Street

BIRD'S OVER THE BULLRING

As well as writing fiction, Mike Chinn can often be seen with his nose in a copy of the Fortean Times. When he supplied the following magazine article, he assured me that Clifton Davies was just a pen name, and that it had originally appeared in the Spring 2005 edition of STRANGE BREW magazine. The fact he had a twitch in his left eye and kept his hands behind his back did, however, make me a little suspicious...

BIRD'S OVER THE BULLRING
by
CLIFTON DAVIES

The Midlands city of Birmingham has seen many changes in fortune. Most recently it has shared the fate of so many of our cities who reached their maturity during the Industrial Revolution: facing the inevitable decline of post-industrial malaise.

Yet the city has not been content to fade into genteel decay, but has reinvented itself on more than one occasion; finding a way to express its future through the past as some of its industrial heritage is saved from destruction and reborn in new plumage. One such place is the Custard Factory: once the home of Bird's Custard, now containing an art gallery, a café, shops and the offices of publishers and local radio. Plus a figure whose natural habitat might be considered far away from the canals and brickwork of a metropolis: the Green Man.

Installed three years ago by Zambian born artist Tawny Gray this sculpture has a corner of the old site to itself where it changes with the seasons (there is living plant life incorporated into it) whilst presiding over visitors. Of her creation, Miss Gray said: *"I've always been interested in the subject since reading the Golden Bough in my teens [...] and when I looked at Birmingham, so heavily bombed in the war and then rebuilt as though cars were its inhabitants rather than humans, I thought it essential to make the Green Man in Digbeth amidst the concrete jungle to remind us that all our egoistic hubris in building cities and sky scrapers will ultimately be reclaimed by the Green Man. There wasn't any particular hook up with Digbeth's particular history [but] I felt that probably, of all places in Birmingham, the Green Man most likely had held sway at some time, somewhere, in Digbeth."*

However, my researches have shown that the Green Man may have "held sway" in the areas around Digbeth until much more recently. Over the years there has been:

- Amorphous shapes lurking along the culverted banks of a local river

- A tree-like figure monopolising a telephone box which melted away to nothing

- Hauntings within the deserted Bird's factory, accompanied by UFO-like phenomena.

- Mysterious phone calls which predicted a disaster.

A brief history of the Bird's Custard Factory

Because his wife was allergic to eggs (the key ingredient used to thicken traditional custard) Alfred Bird first formulated and cooked his substitute in 1837. When he realised the popularity of instant custard, Bird formed *Alfred Bird and Sons Ltd* in Birmingham. By 1895, the company was producing blancmange powder, jelly powder, and egg substitute and the name *Bird's* was already synonymous

with custard powder. During the Great War, *Bird's Custard* was supplied to the British armed forces.

However, World War II saw rationing and serious production limits. During the post-war years *Bird's* became part of the *General Foods Corporation,* which was itself merged into *Kraft Foods* in the 1980s (production had already relocated to Banbury in 1964). In late 2004, *Kraft* sold *Bird's Custard* to *Premier Foods*. From 1964 until 1992, when redevelopment of the old site began, the buildings were deserted (at least of human life) and allowed to sink into dereliction.

High Strangeness in the City

Even though the 1960s was a period of high employment throughout Britain, the Bird's factory languished, the familiar three birds logo on the building's side allowed to fade. But it was not allowed to be forgotten.

In 1972 there occurred the first of many events within the building—a harbinger of the greater oddness to follow. On the evening of 23rd August, bright lights were spotted within the empty factory. A police investigation revealed nothing: no signs of a break-in and no tracks in the dusty floor. The incident was written up and forgotten. Two nights later, on the 25th, just before midnight, more lights were seen. The police once again investigated, and this time the lights persisted long enough for both attending constables—Alan Forbes and John Knowles from Digbeth Police Station —to witness them. PC Forbes described the lights as *"a brilliant white, drowning our flash-lights, drifting above our heads."* PC Knowles added there *"...were three lights in total, although not always 'lit' at the same time, moving at random at an average height of ten feet above the factory floor."* After entertaining the constables for fifteen to thirty minutes (neither man could be sure of the time period involved), all three lights winked out.

This time the event reached a local newspaper and it didn't escape the eye of an anonymous reporter that it was fifty years since the death of Sir Alfred Bird. Was the mournful spirit of the factory's founder returning to bewail the loss of his factory?[1]

There were four more instances of the mysterious "Bird's Lights" as they were now known—on the 27th, 28th and 31st of August, and the 9th September—but other than drifting aimlessly about, the phenomenon did little to excite greater interest. Local "experts" speculated as to their source— ball lightning, phosphorescent insects—but by the time of the final sighting, the lights were forgotten by all but local amateur UFO and ghost investigators.

Then on the night of September the 14th, a bright object was observed moving along Digbeth High Street in a north-south direction. No connection was made with the incidents at the factory and the sighting was relegated to a tiny column-filler in the *BIRMINGHAM EVENING MAIL* under the heading *Flying Saucer over the Bullring.*[2]

For two years all went quiet – or at least, no one reported anything strange. Then in 1974, it all began again, but with distinct differences.

Early in the year (March 3rd[3]) Philip Howard, 35, was walking down Bradford Street—a road that runs parallel to Digbeth High Street—and crossing one of the few spots in the city where the River Rea is not hidden from view. The river is many feet below street level, enclosed by high brick walls and shallow concrete banks at this spot, choked by litter, and is an area unlikely to be used by someone taking an evening stroll. Yet Mr Howard clearly saw, standing on one of the banks, a figure. As it was approximately ten-thirty there was very little in the way of light (the sky was overcast, blocking whatever Moon may have been shining), but Mr Howard was certain of what he saw that night.

"...At first I thought it was a drunk who'd managed to crawl down there. It certainly seemed to be waving about, like it had had one too many. I thought it was staring into the water...

"...Then it kind of looked up at me [...] the whole body sort of twisted to face in my direction. We just stared at each other for a bit [...] then its whole body sort of twisted and flowed, like he was made of hot tar or something. I'd swear it melted – flowed into the water, somehow. Though I don't remember actually seeing it going into the river..." [4]

Although understandably shaken, Mr Howard caught his bus back home (an area known as Springfield, near Hall Green) and went to bed as normal. He never even thought to mention it to his wife, Gloria, for another two days. It was, he said *"...too much like a dream. I couldn't convince myself it had actually happened..."*[5]

And for those who like to connect synchronicities, not only was Mr Howard an ex-employee of Bird's Ltd, but he lost his job when the company moved to Banbury in 1964: exactly ten years earlier.

From then on not only did Mr Howard's odd figure reappear along the banks of the Rea, but it began to haunt the empty Bird's factory, displacing the original lights. And they weren't alone.

• On seven occasions, in 1974 (twice), 1977, 1978, and 1980 (three times) large figures were observed either within the deserted factory (presumably by security staff, but details are sketchy) or in the streets leading off Digbeth High Street. On every occasion the figures are described as tall, dark, lurching (drunkenness is mentioned in three reports), apparently fascinated by some aspect of the building or geography, shaped in a strange manner and vanishing the moment they realise they are being watched. The consensus is that they "melt away" in some manner that none of the (unfortunately anonymous) witnesses can satisfactorily describe.[6] What is notable about all of these sightings is that they took place in broad daylight. Our mystery entity (or entities) was growing confident.

• Two more sightings of Mr Howard's figure by the Rea were reported in 1977 and 1979: again the witnesses report the bulky shape flowed away. Mrs Jeanne Arden—who made her sighting in 1977—described the shape as straddling the river, and draining into it *"...like an oily film."*[7]

• On August 23rd, 1977, a formation of lights in what appeared to be a huge V configuration was observed hovering over the railway viaduct where it crosses Floodgate Street. A crowd of twenty to thirty (again details vary) watched as it slowly drifted west across the High Street in the direction of Balsall Heath. One of the witnesses was said to have compared the sighting to *"...one of them big spaceships from STAR WARS."*[8][9]

• In July 1978, in a telephone box on the corner of Gibb Street, Mr Albert Hall waited impatiently to make a phone call to his mother. The person occupying the phone box didn't seem to be in any hurry; in fact in Mr Hall's words: *"He [was] just standing there, staring at the phone like he hadn't seen one before. I [...] think he was drunk..."* Finally, Mr Hall pulled open the door to ask the person to hurry up and,

again in his words: *"He just vanished – melted into thin air. Though I got the impression he disappeared from the head down ... like he was being rubbed out. [...] Before he vanished I could have sworn I was staring up at a tree with eyes [but] it was so quick, I'm not sure what I saw..."*[10]

Phone Calls and Prophecies

Life for Philip Howard, meanwhile, was becoming intolerable. A year or so after his account had appeared in the *EVENING MAIL*, he started to receive odd phone calls. At first they were just enquiring: asking about his strange encounter and trying to pry more details from him. Mr Howard assumed the caller was either another reporter, someone writing a book about strange phenomena who wanted as many lurid details as he could dig up, or just *"...another flying saucer nut..."* But after a while they took on a darker tone: the caller seemed to want to warn Mr Howard, but was never clear what about. Eventually they became threatening.

Mr Howard had British Telecom change his telephone number, and for a while they ceased; but around the beginning of 1976, they began again.

Curiously, they followed the same pattern as the previous calls: beginning as friendly questions, growing more paranoid and culminating in threats. Once again Mr Howard had the number changed—this time also going ex-directory—but in less than a year, the mysterious caller had found him again.

This time, however, the sequence was different: the calls never became threatening. Instead, after the usual series of tenuous implications of danger to Philip and Gloria Howard, the mystery voice again turned friendly. It said that Mr Howard had passed the test and made three cryptic observations: one, that the Howards would soon *"... reap the rewards of their experiences,"* that Birmingham *"...will rise again from the stultifying dust,"* and *"...before five years are gone, that dust must first destroy."*[11] From that moment on, the phone calls stopped.

Neither Philip nor Gloria Howard had any reason to believe anything the anonymous caller said, and dismissed the ridiculously portentous comments; the couple were simply relieved that the calls had apparently ceased. But just over a month later they received a letter – sent via the offices of the *EVENING MAIL* – from American writer and paranormal researcher Glen Parkes. The letter explained that Parkes was working on a new book— *BEYOND THE VEIL*—and he wished to interview Mr Howard regarding his odd experiences. He even offered a small sum in payment. The Howards were naturally suspicious, especially in the light of the annoying phone calls they had been enduring; Gloria wondered if this Glen Parkes wasn't actually behind them after all: creating a bigger, more sensational story from her husband's original experience. Nevertheless they agreed to meet, at the Howard's home.

The details of that meeting can be found in both *BEYOND THE VEIL* and my own forthcoming book. Peake kept no recordings or transcripts of the conversation— other than noting Philip Howard's verbatim memory of wording of the prophesies (as Peake called them), but I have long felt that the Howards remained wary of the American. I am not sure if they ever believed he knew nothing about the calls before initially contacting them; especially when he claimed to have been a victim of strange messages and Men in Black (MiB) activity himself for some twenty years. But they answered all of Peake's questions in full, convincing him they were genuine— neither holding back nor exaggerating. Peake based an entire chapter on the Howards' experiences, paying them well after *BEYOND THE VEIL* was a considerable, if short-lived, best-seller. It would seem the anonymous caller's first claim—that they would *"reap the rewards of their experiences"*—at least came true.

In 1979, the Howards left Birmingham. Whether they had acquired unwelcome notoriety after the publication of Peake's book, or whether they were rattled by the first "prophecy" appearing to come true, I cannot say. The 1970s had seen the city bloodied by terrorist activity; perhaps the wording— especially of the third prophecy—brought back unpleasant memories. They settled in Leamington Spa—a town to the south of the city of Coventry—and after a brief period of unemployment, Philip Howard bucked the trend and found himself a job. In the Bird's factory in Banbury.

Sadly, the Howards' story did not end there. In 1981 there was an explosion at the factory, caused by dust concentrating into an explosive mixture. Nine were injured, but Philip Howard lost his life in a bleakly ironic interpretation of the last "prophecy".[12]

Dates and Anniversaries

So what are we to make of this tangle of strange events? I have always trodden carefully where the evidence is thin, and even that is anecdotal. Many of the reports of figures within the deserted Digbeth factory are a little light on names, as is the report of the V-shaped formation of lights witnessed by twenty to thirty people. It is possible they are poorly-reported, true events; but it is equally likely they are the invention of a bored reporter who needed to fill a few column inches, basing their tale on earlier, better reported but less fanciful, items.

However, there are some startling correlations with dates. It has already been noted that the first sightings in 1972 occurred fifty years after the death of Sir Alfred Bird, but that is not the only anniversary being celebrated by the Trickster.

• Alfred Hall's melting tree in a telephone box happened one hundred years after the death of Alfred Bird senior: Sir Alfred's father.

• I have already noted that Philip Howard's figure on the Rea made its first appearance ten years after the closure of the Digbeth factory

And in the years since (as the city of Birmingham rose from *"the stultifying dust"*):

• The first phase of the redevelopment of the Custard

Factory began in 1992: twenty years after the first sighting of lights in the factory

• Tawny Gray's Green Man sculpture was installed in 2002 in Gibb Square, not far from Albert Hall's Gibb Street phone box, another twenty years later.

Perhaps it is purely coincidence, but I find it rare that time will allow itself to be parcelled into such neat, round figures.

Was Tawny Gray correct when she said *"...the Green Man most likely had held sway at some time, somewhere, in Digbeth."* And did he, in 1972, start to reassert his dominance? Is this brooding presence meant as homage to this ancient spirit: a way to propitiate him and ensure his blessing as an ancient city regrows? After all, there have been no more reports of lights or oddly-formed figures in the three years since the sculpture was installed.

Clifton Davies is a writer and fortean investigator living in the Midlands. His book, MACABRE MIDLANDS is to be published by Corvid Press in 2006.

[1] Evening Mail, Friday 25th August 1972
[2] Evening Mail, Tuesday 19th September 1972
[3] Evening Mail, Thursday 7th March 1974
[4] BEYOND THE VEIL, Graculus Press 1979
[5] [ibid]
[6] Birmingham Post, Tuesday 14th March 1978
[7] Solihull Times, Friday 1st July 1977
[8] Birmingham Post, Friday 26th August 1977
[9] Express & Star, Friday 2nd September 1977
[10] Solihull Times, Friday 28th July 1978
[11] BEYOND THE VEIL
[12] Oxford Echo, Sunday 31st August 1981

THE DRAGON AND THE GREEN MAN

The Digbeth Dragon, as seen from the Custard Factory courtyard

Since its installation in 1993, a 15 metre-long steel dragon, painted in green and gold acrylic, has been clinging to the wall of the Custard Factory's inner courtyard, glancing down at the pool that lies below. According to the artist Toin Adams, then known as Tawny Gray, the dragon came about simply because she loved dragons:

"Once upon a time I slightly messed around with Digbeth's history in order to justify my choice of the subject. I was at a very boring conference on town planning and I was talking to some planners who asked me why the dragon. In actual fact the name Digbeth was derived from ducks bath in old English. But I mischievously said that there was another more ancient origin which meant dragon's breath... to my amazement some months later I was eavesdropping on a teacher who was taking her class around Digbeth on a day trip and they visited the dragon which had become a bit of a thing for sight seers. Anyway, I heard her telling them the name Digbeth meant dragon's breath!! How funny is that? And I guess much of the small detail in history comes up about in strange and silly ways like this."

And so are urban myths born. Of course, it wasn't long before this guardian totem was joined by a more spectacular companion.

The entrance to the Custard Factory complex has, since 2002, been overlooked by another of Toin's creations—a 12 metre high 'living' sculpture made from stone, fossils and other materials that include snail shells, and vegetation including willow and hawthorn that enable the appearance of the sculpture to change with the seasons. Symbolic of growth and rebirth, the Green Man symbolises the natural evolution of the old architecture into the new, and that, even amidst the urban landscape, the natural world is to be respected and celebrated. Of her most well known creation, Toin had this to say:

"I've always been interested in the subject since reading the Golden Bough in my teens and subsequently coming across mysterious references that echo him in many and various world religions other than

The Green Man, looking down upon Gibb Street

paganism. It's clearly a deeply rooted archetype for mankind. And that does intrigue me. And when I looked at Birmingham, so heavily bombed in the war and then rebuilt as though cars were its inhabitants rather than humans I thought it essential to make the green man in Digbeth amidst the concrete jungle to remind us that all our egoistic hubris in building cities and skyscrapers will ultimately be reclaimed by the green man. A poem by (I think!) Norman Mailer captures something of what inspired me about the green man: 'Today I am proud to say that I am inhuman, that I belong not to men and governments, that I have nothing to do with creeds and principles. I have nothing to do with the creaking machinery of humanity—I belong to the earth! I am the son, the lover. I am her Guardian'.

"There wasn't any particular hook up with Digbeth's particular history although as it was the birthplace of Beorma and so on I felt that probably, of all places in Birmingham, the green man most likely had held sway at some time, somewhere, in Digbeth."

LET SLEEPING WURMS LIE

If you were take a helicopter ride over the Gravelly Hill Motorway Interchange (better known as Spaghetti Junction), you might notice that the sweep of the roads and junctions closely resemble the head of a great sleeping dragon, looking away towards the east, where one of its offspring—the Tyseley Wurm—is said to sleep. Of course, writer Pauline E. Dungate knows a thing or two about dragons and their offspring...

One thing that the people who live and work in Digbeth will tell you is that if you leave the Old Crown untenanted for any length of time there will be trouble.

I didn't intend to get involved—I blame Shelley Wheeler for that. If you don't know Shelley, you're not a Brummie. Go anywhere in the City—the Council House, the clubs, the drop-in centres—and someone will have a tale to tell involving Shelley. She is probably the most tolerant person I know—unless you are a bureaucrat. She has time for everyone except jobsworths, and she has an instinct for knowing when help is needed.

So when, a couple of years ago, she invited me to join her for the St George's Day celebrations, I should've guessed.

At the time, Shelley had an office in the Custard Factory—a Victorian building where once they used to make the powder for *Bird's* that I remember my mother using every week to make the custard for our Sunday lunch. Since its closure they have converted it to a multi-use structure but those sensitive enough can still feels the ghosts of the workers as they walk through what would have been the main entrance to the factory floor.

When I arrived, I was directed up to Shelley's domain. The room was fairly small but stacked with large plastic moving crates overflowing with materials, buttons, beads, hanks of wool and I know not what else. There seemed to be enough to costume the whole of the Handsworth Carnival, not just the one float she said she was equipping. She has a knack of persuading people to give her what she needs and others to do what she wants. Perhaps it's her St. Kitts heritage. I wonder if some kind of Anansi spirit attached itself to her before she was sent to England as a child.

I knocked on her door and entered without waiting. Shelley doesn't stand on ceremony. She was busy texting but the page on her computer screen was an application for some financial grant. She has a knack of getting those, too, for the many projects that spiral around her. She sometimes seems like a motherly spider in the centre of a web, reeling in prizes to hand out to those in need. She glanced up momentarily. "Hi Ellie. Be with you in a moment."

I took the opportunity to look out of the window. There wasn't much of a view but I could just see the railway line that runs on a viaduct south towards Stratford. It was an orientation landmark. I like to have feel of where I am facing.

"That's it," Shelley said with satisfaction.

I decided it was safe to speak. "You didn't invite me just for the parade, did you?"

She had the decency to look abashed. "Well, not quite. I think we've got a problem."

"By we, who do you mean?"

"This neighbourhood."

"What makes you think I can help?"

"You're a witch."

I laughed. "Who have you been talking to?"

She gave me that look then, the one that says don't ask silly questions, the one I remembered from twenty years ago when Shelley was my teacher in Earlswood. "There's been some odd things going on around here."

"What kind of odd?"

"Come along, I'll take you to meet those who've noticed them." She stuffed several things into a large shoulder bag and headed for the door. She locked up and I followed her down to the entrance.

I said the Custard Factory had been converted for multi-purpose use. In the centre of the space that had been part of the factory floor they had constructed a large pool fully equipped with fountain and fish. The complex Shelley's office was in was on one side and opposite was the entrance to a night club. On the wall, appearing to climb it, was a depiction of a ten-foot long metal dragon. It looked good, bronze against white.

"You'd never mistake it for other than it is," Shelley said, "a nicely crafted sculpture."

"No. Who made it?"

"A Zambian artist, I think. Come and meet Vlad. He claims his English is not very good but considering he only arrived from Vilnius six months ago and it's his fourth language, its brilliant."

Shelley headed towards one of the premises at the far end of the ornamental pool. The shutters were down but when Shelley rapped on the outside a young man rolled them up and let us into the dimly lit room. As my eyes adjusted to the dimness the shapes resolved themselves into collapsible bikes. Vlad turned on the lights. "We do not open yet," he said.

Shelley introduced us. "Vlad, this is Ellie. Tell her what you saw on the wall."

"She will not believe me."

"I might," I told him. "I've seen some very strange things."

He looked a little sceptical but said, "This shop. It opens in the night. When club goers do not wish to drive home, one of the workers drives for them. These motor bicycles fold into their trunk so they can get back here. Last week, I stand in the door to watch for customers. I look at the dragon. I like it. It reminds me of legends we have in Lithuania. But this night there were two of them."

"Were they the same?" I asked.

"They were in shape. One was bigger. It was doing a dog thing with the sculpture."

"Mating with it?"

Vlad shrugged. "Maybe it look like that. I went to say to Andrees who works here, come look. It was gone when he came. He did not see it. He think I imagine it."

"Could you have done?"

"I do not know. I do not think so. I know Shelley likes to hear of strange things. I tell her. Now I tell you."

"If it had been one of the customers, I'd've bet on them having had more to drink than they should," Shelley said, "but the people who work here have to stay sober."

"Thank you, Vlad," I said.

"Do you not believe me?"

"I believe you saw something. What it was, I can't be sure."

We left Vlad to close the shop again. I studied the dragon sculpture more closely and wondered how much bigger the reflection would have looked. It wasn't a conventional dragon, more like a monitor lizard with short stubby wings. Further north there were legends of the creature it resembled. I'd not heard tales of one this far south. I made a mental note to consult my copy of *Kear's Mythical Beasts* when I got home.

"Vlad's not the only person to notice odd things," Shelley said.

Almost next door to the Custard Factory complex is what is hailed the Oldest Pub in Birmingham. The building that houses the *Old Crown* is claimed to date from the fourteenth century. The Tudor-style architecture gives a lie to that but stepping inside the ambience gave me a sense of much older foundations beneath it.

Shelley took me round the back where a man in his thirties was stacking prematurely aged bricks. "Hello, Anthony," she said. "You busy?"

"Yes, Miss Shelley. Boss Sean said to tidy yard."

"You are doing a good job. This is Ellie. She'd like to talk to you."

"I must finish this first," Anthony said.

I guessed that Anthony was one of Shelley's protégés. She helped those overlooked for various reasons to find work that suited their abilities. Then kept in touch with them and acted as an intermediary if the need arose.

"We're going to look at the well, Anthony. Come and find me when you've finished here."

"Yes, Miss Shelley." He concentrated on straightening the pile of bricks while we went inside.

The interior of the building was in the kind of mess that often accompanies refurbishment. It all looked half finished and dust cloaked everything. From a distant room came the tinny sound of Radio One on a portable out of sync with the snore of woodcutting. Above us, the original oak beams gleamed with new gloss paint, already speckled with whatever fogged the air. The plaster between them looked damp enough to be newly applied. Shelley headed straight for the room where the sounds activity of were coming from. She turned off the radio.

"Oi!" The carpenter straightened up from his task and glared at her. "What you do that for?"

"So you can hear me when I speak to you," Shelley said sweetly.

He looked her up and down. "And who do you think you are?"

"Anthony's mentor," she said. "You were expecting me."

He seemed a little confused. I would have been in his place. "No-one tol' me. What you do any how?"

"First I ask you how Anthony's getting on, then I talk with Anthony."

The carpenter shrugged. "He's good at cleaning. Does what he's told."

"No problems?"

"Guess not."

"Right. I told Anthony I'd meet him by the well. He wanted to show it to my colleague here."

"Frou there." He pointed towards a low doorway the other side of his workspace. I trailed Shelley through it.

The well was a circular structure some eight bricks high. There was at least one row missing or damaged. They were time worn, the mortar between them crumbling, shedding flakes of grey lime onto the floor. I went and looked down into it. I couldn't see either a gleam of water or the bottom in the darkness.

"They say it's thirty feet deep," Shelley said.

"I'd have expected it to be deeper. Did they use the water for brewing?"

"Probably. It's claimed to be a thousand years old and I wouldn't fancy drinking the water in those days."

"I've finished, Miss Shelley," Anthony said, joining them.

"That's good. Will you tell Ellie what you saw here?"

Anthony looked down at the floor and made an arc in the dust with his toe. "Sean says I imagined it."

"I'd like to know," I said. "I've seen some very strange things. Not everyone believes me either."

There were glances towards the door where Sean had put the radio on again, and at Shelley. "Well… I come here early, see. Sean says he trusts me with a key. As long as I wear it." Anthony took the key on a ribbon from under his shirt to show them. "There is much dust to sweep away. I seen foot prints. Like a rat but bigger. Longer toe marks. I found dead cat all chewed up."

"Is this every day?" I asked.

Anthony shook his head. "Just sometimes. Then I stay late when the walls got scraped. Sean says the dust got to settle so they can paint and it look good."

"What did you see, Anthony?" Shelley prompted him gently.

"It were a dragon. Like the one on the wall. By Miss Shelley's office."

"Where did you see it?" I thought it unlikely to be coincidence that two different people had hallucinated the same thing.

"It came out the well." Anthony stared at us defiantly, then his expression crumpled. "You don't believe me. No-one does."

"Actually, Anthony, I do."

His face lit up. "Then it is real."

"Yes. Shelley, have cats and dogs been going missing in the area?"

"Hard to tell. Not many folks live around here. And there are lots of feral cats."

I walked over to the well again and stared into it. "Anthony, do you ever put anything in the well."

"Oh no. Sean tips his coffee down there sometimes."

I was beginning to get an idea what was going on but I needed to check a few things before I wanted to say anything. "Anthony, would you lend me your key?"

He clutched at the ribbon and shook his head vehemently. "No, no."

"Okay. If I came back in a couple of days, would you let me in and let me stay here at night."

I could almost see his thoughts. He screwed up his face, reviewing what he had been told to see if what I was asking was against the rules.

"You can stay with me," I said.

"Okay."

"Good, man. I'll call Shelley and she can tell you when to expect me."

"Okay."

***

Shelley and I headed into the City Centre for the parade. As she had predicted, I enjoyed myself. I shouldn't have been surprised at the number of people that intersected our path who knew Shelley and wanted to stop and talk to her.

She was in her element.

Three days later I was heading back to Birmingham. I met Anthony at the back of the *Old Crown* just as it was getting dark.

"They will see if we turn the lights on," he said. He seemed a little nervous. I wasn't sure if it was because we were going into the building outside working hours or if it was the darkness that worried him. Being so close to the road, I expected to gat a fair amount of light coming in from the street.

"I have torches. Are you okay in the dark?"

He nodded. "Yes, Miss Ellie."

I handed him one of my torches. "We will have to be quiet if we want to see your animal. If you get worried, squirt it with this." I handed him an atomiser.

"What is in it?"

"Lavender oil. It is harmless to us."

"My grandmother, she says lavender helps her sleep."

"Your grandmother is a wise woman. Would you unlock the door for us, Anthony?"

I didn't insist that he locked it behind us. One of us might want a quick way out. Anthony waved his torch around a lot as he led the way to the room where the well was. I noticed how well swept the floor was compared with my earlier visit. I put my shoulder bag down on the opposite side of the space to the well. That was a relief as some of the contents were quite heavy. "Will you shine that light here, please Anthony?" I said.

He didn't hold it particularly steadily but I was used to getting out what I needed by touch alone. I laid them out on the floor. The largest was a Tupperware box. I opened it carefully so as not to spill the contents. Mostly it was a leg of lamb which had been marinating in beer for the last two days.

"It smells funny," Anthony said.

"I hope it smells good to your dragon."

I placed the hunk of lamb midway between us and the well, with a trail of the juices leading to it. Then we had to wait. Anthony wasn't the kind of person who could sit still for a long time without a purpose so I gave him the task of keeping watch. I fitted red filters to the torches and told him to switch on for a count of two when he heard any strange noise. The creature—I suspected it was a wurm or a horned kow—was unlikely to be deterred by a flash of red, if it even noticed it. Nocturnal creatures disliked bright lights but muted ones didn't seem to cause them discomfort.

I was used to sitting motionless for long periods of time and I refused to let the shufflings Anthony made distract me. He turned on the light twice. Once he illuminated a moth battering against the window; the second time I caught a glimpse of a mouse tail. I think we both heard the scratchings from the well at the same time. It was like the ticking of stone cooling after a day in hot sun. I turned my torch on, too.

It was the tongue I saw first; the long, double fork tasting the air above the rim of the well. The snout followed, moving from side to side. I was sure it sensed us. We would show up as heat sources to the pits beneath the eyes. Long clawed fingers gripped the uppermost row of bricks. Slowly, it hauled itself over the top. Vlad had been right. It did resemble the dragon on the Custard Factory wall. The front feet of the wurm thumped onto the flagged floor. It started towards us with that rolling gait common to all lizards. Except for the stumpy, nascent wings it could have been a large monitor lizard, one approaching the size of a half-grown Komodo Dragon. Like them, this was likely to be fast and have an equally poisonous bite. I hoped Anthony would be able to keep relatively still and quiet, and that it would go for the bait rather than us. In my free hand I raised my lavender spray—just in case.

I needn't have worried. As it opened its mouth to show its double row of sharp teeth, it scented the lamb. The tongue flicked over the surface of the joint. Anthony sneezed. The beast looked up but I heard a hiss as Anthony pressed the button on the lavender spray. As the perfume choked the air, the wurm snatched up the offering and vanished back over the lip of the well with it.

"Sorry," Anthony said.

"'S okay. Just help me with these." I started pulling the cans of beer out of my bag. "Open the cans and pour the contents down the well."

"Won't that make him drunk?"

"In a way. Then he will sleep. Save one can for yourself."

We sat sipping beer and watching the well. I thought I detected the rumble of snoring from underground but that might just have been a bus trundling past.

"No-one will be believe what I saw," Anthony said.

"I do. I saw it too. But if we don't tell, no-one will call us liars."

***

Next time I saw Shelley it was when she invited me to the Handsworth Carnival. I was a little wary of meeting her but she only wanted to know what had gone down at the *Old Crown*.

"Anthony wouldn't tell me," she said.

I smiled. "He didn't want to be called a liar. It was a wurm."

"Will it be back?"

"It hasn't gone away. I just put it back to sleep. Once the place reopens, and as long as the bar serves beer, the aroma of hops will keep it comatose. In the meantime, Anthony will pour beer down the well once a week. There shouldn't be any more bother."

"That's good because there have been some strange sightings up near Sutton Park…."

HIGH STREET DERITEND

Stepping out of Gibb Street and onto the main High Street, the dual carriageway that separates the industrial monoculture of Digbeth in the North from the densely populated areas known as Cheapside and Highgate. This has been the principal route into the town since the twelfth century, at which time it was a dirty, dusty Holloway, with both sides being fully developed by the early eighteenth century. The High Street is divided into three stretches—Digbeth, towards the city centre, defined by the profile of the starkly columnal Rotunda and the Bullring's iconic Selfridge Building (variously known as the armadillo, the beehive or the beached whale), Deritend, bridging the River Rea and an oxbow brook long since buried under the road, and Bordesley, heading out of the town towards Camp Hill and the eastern fringes of Birmingham.

DERITEND

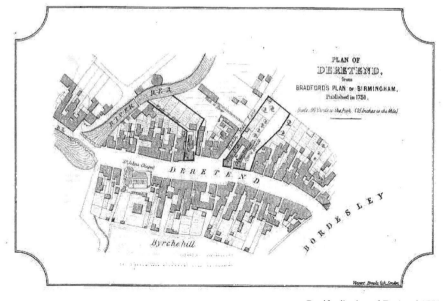

The name Deritend harks back to the early origins of the area as a place where woodland and flatland came together on the banks of the River Rea. First set down as *Duryzatehende* in 1381, there is some debate over whether its origin is from the Celtic *dwr* meaning 'water' combined with the Anglo-Saxon *geat*, meaning 'gate', or whether it

Bradford's plan of Deritend 1751.

comes from an entirely Anglo-Saxon phrase, *deor geat*, meaning deer gate.

The latter name suggests that the area was the deer gate end of the de Birmingham family's deer park (allowing the passage of small animals, but not de Bermingham's deer), much of which was sold in the twelfth century to make way for medieval burgage plots which occupy that part of Digbeth which is closest to the town centre. The original boundary is recalled by Park Street, once called *Le Parkestrete* and *Overparkstret*, and the area was chosen because water the water of the area—pools, springs, wells and of course, the River Rea itself—were essential to emerging industry.

As a grazing site crossing the Rea, it would certainly have been a good crossing point between the hamlet and the park beyond. When John Leland came to Birmingham in 1538 he referred, in a letter to Henry VIII, to the area as Dyrtey (pronounced 'dirty'):

"This strete, as I remember, is caullyd Dyrtey, in it dwelle smithes and cuttelers, and there is a brooke that devydithe this strete from Bremisham. Dyrtey is but an hamlet or membre longynge to the paroche therby and is clene seperated from Bremischam paroche."

This gave rise to the area being known locally as 'the dirty end'.

THE GOLDEN LION

The Golden Lion, Bordesley.

The *Golden Lion*, on the opposite side of the High Street, was a sixteenth century inn which is originally believed to have been the Clergy House and School of the Guild of Deritend. It is said that during the time before it became an Inn, the premises was used by John Rogers to print his Matthew Bible.

The original location of the *Golden Lion* makes it a prime candidate for being the site of the first casualty of the Battle of Kempe's Hill (Another is the *Old Swan Inn*, long-since demolished). It is said that an ostler named Thomas stepped out from one of these coaching inns onto the road with the intention of greet the King's troops and taking their horses. He was instead cut down and killed.

The *Golden Lion* was eventually relocated to Cannon Hill Park in Edgbaston in 1911 to make way for redevelopment. Since being moved there the building has fallen into disrepair. In spite of this Birmingham City Council make periodic plans to relocate the inn to its original home in Deritend.

ST. JOHN'S CHAPEL & JOHN ROGERS, MARTYR

Portrait of John Rogers by Willem van de Passe alongside Frontispiece of the *Matthew Bible* and St. John's Chapel, Deritend.

Opposite the *Old Crown* on what is now the Bull Ring trading estate you will find three blue plaques that stand on the site of the old chapel of St. John, which had been established by the Lollard supporters of John Wycliffe in 1375. It was needed because the inhabitants of Deritend and Bordesley were prone to being cut off from their parish church in Aston whenever the River Rea flooded.

Another of these plaques commemorates the Martyrdom of John Rogers, the first English Protestant martyr to die during the reign of the Catholic Queen Mary, in February 1555.

Born in Deritend in 1505 and schooled by the Guild of St. John in the school that is now known as the *Old Crown* public house, Rogers was the son of a lorimer and the grandson of a tanner, who became a clergyman and, under the pseudonym Thomas Matthew, built upon the works of William Tyndale and Myles Coverdale to translate and publish a complete English Bible—known as the *Matthew Bible*—adapted directly from Greek and Hebrew texts in 1537.

Rogers abhorred both papists and radical protestants alike, and was arrested as a Lollard, excommunicated and sentenced to death for heresy. He was burned at the stake in Smithfield, London, leaving behind a wife and eleven children. Some later sources have misinterpreted this, suggesting he may have died in his native Warwickshire, outside the Smithfield meat market at the city end of Digbeth.

The site of the chapel of St. John the Baptist (currently occupied by Mucklow's *Bull Ring Trading Estate*) had, during World War II, been the site of heavily bombed factory, *Thomas, Haddon & Stokes*, whose cellar was said to have been haunted by a man subsequently said to be Rogers himself, lamenting the chapel's demise. The fact that this ghost has not been seen since the plaques commemorating the chapel's existence, and his own death, were put in place, is cited as evidence of this.

HEATH MILL LANE

Moving away from the city centre and up the hill towards Bordesley and Camp Hill, the High Street comes to a junction with Heath Mill Lane, which recalls a time when the River Rea flowed openly through the area, cutting both the High Street and Floodgate Street in two. Heath Mill Lane was named for a Water Mill used for grinding corn since 1532 (prior to this the street had been Cooper's Mill Lane). While no water mills survive, at its industrial peak there were more than twenty, initially for the grinding of corn into flour but there were also forge-mills which, during the Civil War, were put to use for the making of sword blades for the Commonwealth army.

DERITEND FREE LIBRARY AND LLOYD'S BANK

Originally the Southern District Library, this Gothic building is one of three free libraries that opened on the same day on 28th October

1866 (the others being Birmingham's first Central Reference Library and the Eastern District Library in Gosta Green, both of which have now disappeared). It closed in 1940 and was refurbished in 2002 before being incorporated into the Custard Factory complex.

At some point the Library was combined with the adjacent building—one of the earliest branches of *Lloyds Bank*, c.1874, which was only a short trap ride away from the Lloyd family's rural retreat at Owens Farm in what is now a very urban Sparkbrook. *Taylor & Lloyd* had operated out of Dale End in Birmingham until, in the wake of the suicide of James Taylor in 1853, the business reformed as *Lloyd's Bank Ltd* in 1865. Several branches were soon opened, including that in Heath Mill Lane which bears the the original company logo—that of a

The old Free Library, Deritend and the original Lloyd's beehive logo.

beehive representing work and hardship. This had first been adopted by *Taylor & Lloyd* in 1822 following the theft of banknotes on the London to Birmingham mail route (to help trace stolen notes in future, a more distinctive image was required). This logo was replaced by the famous black horse in 1884, but remained in use until the bank relocated to London in 1911.

THE OLD CROWN

One of the few medieval buildings remaining in Birmingham, legend has it that the *Old Crown* was built in 1368 by a resident of the area called Robert O' the Green. Who Robert was remains a mystery, but it may be no coincidence that the *Birmingham & Midland District of the Ancient Order of Foresters*, founded in 1843, first held court at the inn.

It is generally believed, however, that the present *Old Crown* dates from around 1492—at around the same time that the *Saracen's Head* in King's Norton was built. There are earlier foundations, but this building began life as a School built in the fifteenth century by the Guild of St. John. Only the first floor and part of the ground floor façade remain, the rest of the building having been reworked over the years. When the Guild dissolved in 1549 it passed into the hands of Richard Smallbroke, an attorney whose name is associated with other parts of Birmingham.

The Old Crown at Heath Mill Lane.

The Old Crown Well

A sketch of the Old Crown in 1863, from *Memorials of Old Birmingham*.

Remarked upon by John Leland in 1538 as "a fair mansion of tymber" to King Henry VIII, whose daughter Elizabeth was herself a patron of the Inn, resting there in 1575 following a trip to nearby Kenilworth Castle. It is perhaps this Royal connection that enabled the building to survive the Battle of Kempe's Hill some years later.

As a working Inn the *Old Crown* has an a la carte restaurant, a bar and eight bedrooms. Like many of the early buildings in Digbeth, it comes with its own well, 30 feet deep and said to have been sunk a thousand years ago. It is also haunted. The spirit of a white lady has sometimes been seen passing between the well and the bar, where another spirit is said to wander, passing from the bar (where he occasionally taps the bar staff on the shoulder in the hope of getting served), through the wall, and into the restaurant. The spirit of a Victorian drayman, replete with sideburns and a bowler hat, has also been seen in the beer cellar, resting upon a barrel between the loading and unloading of his beer and spirits.

Other incidents, including a strange white mist in the master bedroom and loud ghostly banging from the roof, have made the inn a popular haunt for ghost-hunters.

ROBERT O' THE GREEN & THE POOR KNIGHT

Howard Pyle's Robin Hood, 1883.

Part of writer Julius Horne's legacy was a weathered, hand-typed manuscript containing the following story. The principals are very obviously Robin and his Merry Men, and the plot bears a striking resemblance to a modern English translation of the original child ballad A Geste of Robyn Hode published between 1492 and 1534. It also fits neatly into the story of the Old Crown and several nearby locations, so perhaps it reveals the true identity of Robert O' the Green. Is it a translation of an earlier story, or is it an early mash-up? Only Julius knew for sure...

L egend tells of Robert, a King's yeoman, and his company, who took upon themselves a greenwood meadow on the Holloway leading into Brymicham, a market town recovering from the ravages of plague and fire. Once outlawed, they had taken old King Edward's pardon, fighting his wars in France until they tired of service, taking up their old ways and returning north through the forest of Arden and along the old Watlinge Street. Stopping over to trade at the town's Michaelmas market, they chose to stay awhile.

Robert put his company to good use as workers on the hill. The first of his men, a former tanner called Scarlet—after the fine red hides he once cut and dyed—took up work at the tanyards; the second, a giant of a man called John the Nailer, took up the forge-hammer of his youth; the third, the son of a miller, made good at one of the corn-mills that lined the river close by. His men would toil in the mornings and work timber in the afternoon, building themselves a well-thatched ale lodge set about an ancient well.

In all this time Robert and his men were known to be good and courteous to all within the town. Proud of their handiwork, but keen to return to their old ways, it was John the Nailer who spoke first.

"Master, we should hold ourselves a feast to celebrate our achievements. We should take ourselves some beer and hunt the King's venison. It would do us much good."

Robert declined. "I cannot eat for my own reward, and I cannot take from those we work beside. We need an unworthy patron who can afford to give us custom. A knight perhaps, or a wealthy baron, who can stand to feed both ourselves and our neighbours."

"Where would you have us find such a man?" asked Scarlet. "And how shall we persuade him? With arms? We can beat him, bind him and bring him here to you."

"There shall be no force," said Robert. "And we should be careful who we choose. No honest worker. No husband or yeoman or squire who might turn out to be a good fellow. But a bishop, or an archbishop, a knight, a shreve or a tallager from beyond this manor. They should be the type of men we seek."

"You have our word on it," said John. "We shall find ourselves an unworthy guest, and we shall all dine together."

"Then take up your bows," said Robert. "And take yourselves up along the Tame, and so to Watlinge Street. Perchance you will meet him there."

And so the three yeomen set off towards the north and east, beyond the Rea and along the Tame, resting at the bow-bearer's lodge before they came to Watlinge Street, whereupon they hid themselves and lay in wait for their quarry. A full three hours they waited until, as the sun began to set, a knight came riding by.

It was dark and it was dreary when the yeomen stood before their prey. The knight before them was dressed simply, with thin raiment and only a single stirrup upon his horse. His draped hood covered a worn and sorry face and his sword and shield were dulled and pitted. No knight could have looked in more sorry a state.

It was John the Nailer who stood before him, affecting a low and courteous bow.

"Welcome, gentle knight," he said. "Welcome to the greenwood. My master bids you join us, for he fasts while waiting upon your attendance."

"Your Master," the Knight replied. "Who might he be?"

Scarlet said, "Robert. Robert O' the Green."

"I know the name," said the knight. "A good yeoman, and a once-made knight himself. I had planned to dine at the Coleshill Manor" he said, "but it pleases me to come with you."

They led the knight back to Brymicham, and upon seeing the

Holloway and the newly fashioned ale lodge, tears of joy ran down his cheeks. There, in its doorway, stood Robert O' the Green.

"Welcome, Sir knight," said Robert, doffing his cap and bowing low to his guest. "I have spent many hours fasting in anticipation of your company."

The knight returned the yeoman's bow, thanking Robert and his company for their kind offer. Ushering his guest inside, the yeoman joined him in washing before settling down to dinner. The hall was set for a feast not far removed from that which might be offered in a manor or a castle. Around the table were the villeins and the tenants of the Holloway, and laid before them were ale and poultry of all kinds, bread and wine, fruit and sweets, and diverse cuts of royal venison, laid out as if for King Edward himself.

"Such a feast, sir," said the knight, taking up his seat at Robert's table. "Gramercy. I have not seen such a feast for many weeks, and my journey home has been a long one. Should I pass this way again I must return your favour, and provide you with as good a dinner as I see here."

"Gramercy to you also, Sir knight," said Robert. "I have never been more hungry, nor ever prepared a meal like this before."

And so the knight, the yeomen and the workers of Brymicham set about their dinner with great relish. The ale flowed, the food diminished and at last the dinner was done. With the feast drawing to a close and the townsfolk ready to depart, Robert's guest stood to take his leave.

"I pray you," said his host. "It is only right and proper, I think, that you should settle for the meal. It has never been the custom, as I see it, for a yeoman to make payment for a knight."

Drawing up his hood, the knight hung his head. "I have nothing in my coffers," said he. "I am but a poor knight, for my shame."

"John, Scarlet, go and look," said Robert to his men. "And leave nothing unchecked."

"Now, tell me truth,' said the yeoman as his company searched through the knight's possessions. "God help you if you have lied in this matter—"

"I swear to you, by God, that I have no more than ten shillings to my name."

"And you have no more?"

"Not one penny," said the knight. "I am but a poor knight in the service of Saint John."

"He speaks the truth," said John the Nailer. Entering the lodge, he set the knight's mantle upon the table. Spreading it out he revealed the knight's coffer.

Robert opened the box, wherein he spied nothing more than a handful of groats.

"It is true indeed," he said, embracing the knight and dismissing his companions. "Now, sir, you must tell me one thing, and I shall keep your counsel. I trust you were made a knight of force, or else were raised up from the yeomanry? Or were you simply a poor husband? A gambler? A drinker? A usurer? Or simply a poor manager of your affairs? What wrong has led you to this?"

"None of those things," said the knight. "I swear by God that my father was a knight, and his before. I am a man disgraced and only God in heaven can help me now.

"Before I left these shores I had good money, calling upon four hundred pounds or more to my name."

"Now have I nothing," said the knight. "God himself has brought me to such an end, but—for my children and my wife, I must find a way to make amends."

"You must tell me how you lost your riches."

"My son, Robert. He that should have been my heir. He stood as my squire at Cressy, and when we both fell prisoner to the French I arranged to secure his freedom through the sale of goods. My own ransom was too great a price to pay, and so I gave myself up to secure his release. Now I am freed I find the ransom went unpaid and that my son died in captivity. My lands, meanwhile, were forfeit to the church."

"Sir," Robert cursed. "What shall befall you if you lose your land?"

"A pilgrimage," said the knight. "Across the ocean to see where Christ died upon the mount of Calvary; for I cannot reclaim my family without it. I may as well go there before I die."

"Farewell, friends," said the knight as tears rain from his eyes, turning to be on his way.

"Wait, friend," said Robert. "What about your friends?"

"I had plenty when I was landed, but now I am shunned and ignored. My favour has faded with my fortune."

Summoning his company, Robert ordered flagons to be filled with wine. He, John, Scarlet and the miller's son then made a toast to the knight.

"You have friends here," said Robert. "For within this lodge may you find good cheer. Our time in Arden is almost at an end, and while we cannot restore your manor, we can at least see you right."

"What is it you propose?" asked the knight.

"I am not suited to the landed life," said Robert. "John, bring forward my treasury!"

The Nailer did as Robert bade, returning with the yeoman's own coffer, which he duly opened, Counting out four hundred pounds, the yeoman dropped it into the knight's coffer.

"The lodge is yours," said Robert. "The money you shall use to reunite your family, and in return, I ask but one favour."

"By God," said the knight, in awe of his host's generosity. "You cannot—"

"It is but alms to help a poor knight that is fallen into poverty," said Robert. "And in return I ask only that you rededicate your life to Saint John, and that you serve the villeins and the tenants of this parish as I had planned to do."

The knight knelt before the yeoman, and pledged that it would be so.

"And you," asked the knight. "What of Robert O' the Green?"

"John shall fix your arms and Scarlet will restore your livery. Then we shall be on our way—from the Green we came, and to the greenwood we shall return."

HIGH STREET, BORDESLEY

Beyond the *Old Crown* lies High Street Bordesley. A distinct hamlet in the parish of Aston rather than Birmingham, Bordesley was characterised by a number of open fields, and remained separated from Deritend and Digbeth until it was incorporated with the Municipal Borough of Birmingham in 1838. It was here that the armies of Prince Rupert gathered for the early part of the Battle of Bordesley Bridge (See *Appendix I: The Battle of Kempe's Hill*). Its manor, Bordesley Hall, stood high upon the hill until it was burned down in the riots of 1791.

Street view of High Street, Bordesley, looking uphill towards Camp Hill.

William Hutton (bottom) Dr. Joseph Priestley (top).

THE CHURCH & KING RIOTS

Also called The Priestley Riots, these disturbances were triggered by the second anniversary of Bastille Day. A meeting of well-to-do entrepreneurs, non-conformists and free thinkers met for a dinner to commemorate the French revolution. This caused those who feared the possibility of an English Revolution to provoke members of Birmingham's own working classes to march against those 'dissenters' who might encourage such thinking.

Digbeth itself was spared from violence, being the home of many of the rioters. On the first day—July 14th—a drunken mob smashed windows where the non-conformists met, shouting 'Church & King for ever!' in protest against what was perceived as a plot by dissenters.

The Priestley Riots, from Cassell's *History of England*, 1890 (left) Rioters burning Dr. Priestley's House on 14th July 1791, from the Susan Lowndes Marques Collection. (right)

The rioters burned down the New Meeting House of Dr. Joseph Priestley, the scientist and Unitarian minister targeted by the mob as the main dissenter against the crown. After wrecking parts of the town they marched out through Digbeth and up towards Camp Hill, where they set fire to Priestley's home and laboratory, Fair Hill, forcing him to flee to New York, never to return.

On the second day William Hutton, chronicler of Birmingham's History, attempted to protect his own premises—a booksellers in High Street, Dale End—by borrowing from neighbours to bribe the rioters, first with money and then with 329 gallons of ale. He thus saved the shop, but his house in Washwood Heath did not fare so well (His experiences were recorded in a narrative of the riots published in 1816).

Bordesley Hall was burned to the ground that day, along with a dozen other targeted buildings. By the fourth day a troop of 64 hussars force-marched from Nottingham, broke up the riots and restored order to the town.

DIGBETH TYRE

At the end of the nineteenth century a brick-built chapel with a distinctive campanile tower was constructed between the High Street and the Bordesley viaduct. Intended for use as a basilican chapel for St. Edmund's Boys' Home, the building was never consecrated as its builder, Father John Lopes, converted to Catholicism before its completion in 1915. It had a variety of secular uses until, in recent years, it has become a car wash and tyre depot.

Father Lopes' Folly.

THE BROWN LION INN & THE ASTON GAOL

A hundred yards or so beyond the Rainbow and Adderley Street, at the site of 131-148 High Street, Bordesley, the Prison of the Manor of Aston was built in 1733 in a basement to the rear of a pub known as the *Brown Lion Inn*. Intended to serve only as a temporary lock-up prior to appearing in court, the cells were expanded in 1757, but inspections carried out towards the end of the eighteenth century noted how revolting the conditions were, and according to Showell's *Dictionary of Birmingham* in 1885:

"Bordesley Prison, otherwise 'Tarte's Hole' (from the name of one of the keepers), situate in High Street, Bordesley. It was classed in 1802 as one of the worst gaols in the kingdom. The prison was in the backyard of the keeper's house, and it comprised two dark, damp dungeons, twelve feet by seven feet, to which access was gained through a trapdoor, level with the yard, and down ten steps. The only light or air that could reach these cells (which sometimes were an inch deep in water) was through a single iron-grated aperture about a foot square. For petty offenders, runaway apprentices, and disobedient servants, there were two other rooms, opening into the yard, each about twelve feet square. Prisoners' allowance was 4d. per day and a rug to cover them at night on their straw. In 1809 the use of the underground

rooms was put a stop to, and the churchwardens allowed the prisoners a shilling per day for sustenance. Those sentenced to the stocks or to be whipped received their punishments in the street opposite the prison, and, if committed for trial, were put in leg-irons until called for by 'the runners'. The place was used as a lock-up for some time after the incorporation, and the old irons were kept on show for years."

Other accounts suggest that the gaol was known as 'Brownell's Hole', named after either the keeper, Mr. W.D.Brownell, or his wife, Jemima, who were paid for the prisoners' food and drink out of their daily allowance. The closure of the *Brown Lion's* 'underground rooms' corresponds to when the housing of felons was transferred to new cells situated at the Moor Street Public Office.

THE RAINBOW & ADDERLEY STREET

Turning back into Digbeth from the High Street we enter Adderley Street which, despite appearances, is a hub of night-time activity centred around the *Rainbow*, which has been transformed from a street-corner local into a music venue that extends along the road right up to the Bordesley viaduct.

There was a time when nearly every street corner in Digbeth had a local pub. While most, like the *Rainbow* were built for the express purpose, many others were converted to accommodate the needs of the locals. The adaptability of the area's pubs kept many alive even when the residents moved out and the industry dwindled.

The Rainbow at Adderley Street.

Rebuilt on the site of an earlier public house c.1875, the *Rainbow* has undergone little physical change on the outside, but its soul has been influenced by the events that surround it.

In its early days, the tavern (along with the *Wagon & Horses* further along) was a known haunt of the Adderley Street Gang, better known as the Peaky Blinders (*see Appendix II: Law & Order*). In 1890 one of its earliest murders took place when a crowd of Peakies set upon and fractured the skull of an innocent bystander with steel-toed boots. It remained associated with the gang into the early part of the twentieth century, and by the 1950s, the clearance of much of the old housing and the subsequent designation of the area as industrial changed its clientèle.

In the 1990s it was an old local struggling to survive as the pubs around it closed one by one. Then, in 2000, it was rocked by a killing spree carried out by it's odd-job man Philip Smith (*This triple murder is given in more detail in Appendix II: The Birmingham Bigfoot*).

Like a phoenix, the *Rainbow* rose from the ashes, surviving the decline of the traditional industries around it and embracing the rise of Digbeth as a 'creative quarter'. Surrounded by live music venues, the *Rainbow* slowly encroached upon the surrounding area, weathering an abrasive noise abatement row to make bigger and bolder improvements, expanding into its own car park to create the *Rainbow Warehouse*, turning its cellar into a separate music venue, creating a mezzanine layer above the back yard and expanding beyond the railway arches to incorporate what was once *Air*, the biggest indoor rave venue in Britain, with a capacity of 5,000.

UPPER TRINITY STREET

Continuing along Adderley Street, the first right turn brings us to Upper Trinity Street, which heads out of Deritend and into Bordesley proper. On one side of the street is the viaduct itself, which leads to the old Bordesley Cattle Station (its original GWR signage remains intact) which still exists and is used as a storage depot under the viaduct. It was originally used to unload livestock for transport to market. The animals would be herded down to Adderley Street then across to Great Barr Street where they would be driven along the far side of the Grand Union Canal as far as the Proof House Junction. Here they would pass over the canal via a cattle walk which would lead them down to Fazeley Street and across to the Smithfield Meat Market.

Part of the unmanned station remains in use for match-day

traffic as it is the nearest station to the St. Andrew's football stadium. It is after this station that the viaducts divide into two—the Bordesley Viaduct, on which the old Oxford to Birmingham line passes through Digbeth and into Moor Street Station—and the Duddeston Viaduct, better known as the 'Viaduct to Nowhere'.

DUDDESTON VIADUCT—THE VIADUCT TO NOWHERE

Stretching for some 325 metres between Upper Trinity Street and Great Barr Street to the north is the Duddeston Viaduct, a railway folly created as a result of the bitter railway feuds of the 1840s.

In 1838 the *London & Birmingham Railway* (LBR) reached Birmingham, terminating at Curzon Street. A few years later they, along with several other rail companies, merged to form the *London & North Western Railway* (L&NWR), whose major competitor was the *Great Western Ralway* (GWR).

Parliament required L&NWR and GWR to jointly fund the building of a connecting viaduct between the Oxford to Birmingham Line and Curzon Street. Shortly afterwards, before the work commenced, Parliament authorised the building of two new central stations—New Street and Snow Hill. The two companies battled over who would control these stations, and by the end of their negotiations there was no practical need for the viaduct to be built.

However, because the requirement for the viaduct was required by an act of Parliament, L&NWR took legal action to ensure that GWR

A ghost sign close to the site of the Bordesley Cattle Station.

The start of the Duddeston viaduct at Upper Trinity Street (upper right), the end of the Duddeston viaduct at Liverpool Street (below left) and the viaduct's abrupt end where four streets meet (below right).

completed its half of the viaduct. Work commenced in 1848, ending in 1853 when the viaduct reached the boundary of the L&NWR's property.

The unfinished viaduct remains a popular source of innovative ideas, with campaigns to turn it into a high-level urban walkway similar to the New York Highline, providing a concealed park and viewing platform that might one day serve visitors to the city. As with many such ideas, there are dozens of people waiting to take credit if it ever happens.

GREAT BARR STREET & FAZELEY STREET

Great Barr Street provides the back way in and out of the city, its hump-backed bridge leading out of Digbeth and Deritend towards the ring road and the industrial landscape of east Birmingham. It is here, marked by an old Victorian toilet on one side of the junction, and by the old *Forge Tavern* on the other, that the Duddeston Viaduct ends, and the Grand Union Canal, running parallel with Fazeley Street, begins.

Known as Lake Meadow Hill before the canals and the railways came, Fazeley Street has become the principal route into the heart of industrial Digbeth, once lined with canal-side wharves and loading warehouses on one side of the road, and a mix of back-to-back courtyards and factories on the other.

The Great Barr Street bridge, where road, viaduct and canal meet.

THE FORGE TAVERN

The *Forge Tavern* is perhaps the last of Digbeth's truly local locals, proudly sitting on the junction of Fazeley and Great Barr Streets,

The view along Fazeley Street, past the old Unitarian chapel that is now Fazeley Studios.

opposite a listed Victorian urinal and beside an indoor go-kart track hidden from view by the brick façade that keeps most of Digbeth's secrets. Being only a short walk from St. Andrew's football ground, it is a Blues pub that serves up cheap beer and cheap food to the local community rather than targeting those more interested in the area's cultural or creative scene.

FAZELEY STUDIOS & THE BOND COMPANY

The Custard Factory is not alone in providing workspace for Birmingham's creative community. With its own wharf and enclosed courtyard leading

The Forge Tavern.

out onto the Grand Union Canal, the Bond Company competes (once a Victorian bonded warehouse and ice store) with other workspace providers to house creative businesses. On the opposite side of Fazeley Street is a renovated Unitarian Mission Church that briefly housed the *Ikon Eastside* gallery, and which now, as Fazeley Studios, provides yet more creative studio space.

Together these sites, the Custard Factory and other managed workspaces scattered across the area have helped to transform Digbeth from weathered industrial monoculture into a fledgeling urban village.

Fazeley Studios alongside The Bond Arch and The Bond, Icehouse entrance.

THE WARWICK BAR & THE GRAND UNION CANAL

The stretch of canal running behind Fazeley Street was once the end of the Warwick and Birmingham Junction Canal (c.1844) which was built to connect with the Digbeth Branch Canal (c.1799). It was the principal route used to bring goods like fruit (at the Banana Warehouse), tea (at Typhoo Wharf) and ice (bound for the cold stores at the Bond and on Digbeth High Street) into the centre of Birmingham, with wharves originally lining the road-side of the canal to accommodate loading and unloading. It was also a deciding factor for the location of industrial steam mills and coal wharves to the area at the beginning of the nineteenth century. It became part of the Grand Union Canal in 1929, and there are a number of features unique to Digbeth.

The Grand Union Canal alongside The Warwick Bar.

THE RIVER REA

Siphoned for mills, culverted, flood-gated and storm-drained, there is very little of the original River Rea visible overground. The source of the river lies twelve miles to the south of Birmingham in the Waseley Hills Country Park. It then passes through the Lickey Hills and into Northfield before passing through Cannon Hill Park into Balsall Heath and Highgate. It then enters Digbeth where it is little more than a shallow culverted stream that runs beneath Floodgate Street and the canal aqueduct.

Barely accessible from the canal tow-path, this secluded part of the Rea, known as Back Brooke, has been well known for lunch time and night-time assignations over the years, disappearing under the city's ring road before joining the River Tame beneath spaghetti junction two miles to the north-east.

The Rea's Back Brook passes beneath the Grand Union Canal.

MONTAGUE STREET

On the opposite side of the canal to Fazeley Street is a steep embankment built up to conceal what was once a landfill site that lies behind it. Once the headquarters of Birmingham's Environmental Services, its Montague Street Depot is a hidden island in the heart of Birmingham. Large enough to contain a small village, it was previously the city's Cattle and Pig Market, established in 1892. It was joined to the Smithfield Meat Market at the top of Digbeth by a cattle walk connecting it to Fazeley Street where Warwick Bar and the Proof House Junction come together.

FELLOWS, MORTON & CLAYTON

An unusual building visible in profile from the tow-path is the *Fellows Morton & Clayton* boatyard, which clearly takes the shape of one of the boats it was renowned for building. The company first made its headquarters in Fazeley Street in 1890, but the present building was built in 1935. It served as the company's base of operations until it wound up in 1948. When in use the boatyard was served by an inlet and wharves that would allow newly constructed boats to pass out onto the canal.

Fellows, Morton & Clayton's the old narrowboat yard shaped like an old narrowboat.

THE BANANA WAREHOUSE

Directly opposite the Warwick Bar stop lock is the overhanging canopy of the Warwick Bar Warehouse erected c.1850. A century later it came under the ownership of *Geest*, who used it to import and store bananas in from the Windward Islands. As the last major use of the warehouse before it fell into disrepair, it has retained its identity as the banana warehouse ever since.

The Former Geest Banana Warehouse at
Warwick Bar.

THE PROOF HOUSE TURN

The rear of the Gun Barrel Proofing House compound backs onto the Proof House canal junction which connects the Typhoo Canal Basin to the Digbeth Branch Canal and Warwick Bar. The name of the junction is shared with the Proof House Railway Junction that lies between the canal and New Street Station.

The Proof House junction at the rear of the Gun Barrel Proofing House.

TYPHOO BASIN & THE BIRMINGHAM BLITZ

Passing beneath Fazeley Street, the Digbeth Branch Line comes to an end at what was originally called Bordesley Street Wharf. Serving steam mills, rolling mills and timber yards, it eventually passed into the hands of the Birmingham-based *Typhoo Tea Company,* who built new premises on Bordesley Street in 1924, using the canal to bring in three thousand crates of Ceylon tea per week. This would be stored in a bonded warehouse on site until import duty was paid.

Everything changed when the Luftwaffe targeted Birmingham for a heavy bombing campaign between 1940 and 1943. As the third most bombed city in Britain (after London and Liverpool), the city's industrial areas were, particularly those in close proximity to water features such as the Grand Union Canal, most at risk. The Typhoo factory was hit by incendiary bombs on 10th April 1941, destroying much of the complex, but leaving its front façade reasonably intact.

There are many tales of unexploded bombs beneath the site, and the extensive damage caused is often cited as the reason why Typhoo ended its tea packing operations there in 1978. Since then, much of the site remains unused.

Fazeley Bridge passes between the Proof House Turn and Typhoo Wharf (above) The Typhoo Basin (below).

THE ANORAK

When is a ghost story an urban fantasy? We find out in this contemporary tale, when one of Digbeth's more colourful local historians puts in a brief cameo appearance.

"I was walking home," said Sandra, "from the *Black Horse* back to Bordesley. I don't like walking alone, but in those days I'd rather have walked along the tow-path than down through Digbeth itself."

Sandra Maloney had been a barmaid at the time, and this was the first time she had been properly interviewed since the incident happened in the summer of '92. In her early forties, she had given up bar work in favour of some cleaning work up at Aston University. Same general location, different job.

"You know the area well?" I asked, sketching out a small map as we spoke. I'm not a policeman, but in my line of work it's essential to both record an interview and to take written notes at the same time. The notes are for random thoughts and as an aide memoir to make sure I ask all the right questions, but the tape... that's researcher's gold.

"Very well," she nodded. "It's not far for me, and I've no kids so I've never had to move or anything. I grew up around here.

"I'll probably end up haunting the place too," she laughed nervously, drawing on her third cigarette in what felt like as many minutes. She was short, maybe five feet two, with a gaunt figure and cropped mousey brown hair. Her skin was weathered and her teeth yellowed by years of nicotine abuse.

"So why haven't you told anyone about this before?" I asked. "Twenty years is a long time to wait."

"Oh, I've told anyone down the pub that'll buy me a drink," she said, "but its never really been something I thought was worth more than a lager dash."

"So, what time was it? And the weather?"

"The weather? Christ knows. It was dark, and my shift was done, so a bit after midnight. The sky must have been clear because if I couldn't see well enough I'd have waited an hour and cadged a lift. It's only a twenty minute walk, tops, and there's never many on the canal at that time, especially midweek."

"You remember the day?"

"Tuesday or Thursday most likely. Those were my shifts. The

tramps hung out under arches nearer the city centre, and the rent boys only lurked on the cut on Friday or Saturday nights."

"Rent boys?"

"Yeah," she stubbed her cigarette and pulled out another. "Down by the culvert, where the Rea goes under the canal, there's some wilderness. It's so far from anywhere else on a weekend that the coppers never check it out. Punters come down from the slipper sometimes, but usually it's the closeted ones that sneak out of the local pubs or at the end of a metal-bashing shift."

"The slipper?"

"Old name for the Gay Quarter," she said, taking another drag. "More of a triangle back then. *Jester* and the *'gale* across to the *Vic*, and then down Hurst Street."

I knew where she meant. That part of town had many names because it overlapped with Chinatown and the theatres. Southside is the latest label.

"So, you left the *Black Horse* at around midnight, and then?"

"The canal runs behind the pub, so I could slip onto the tow-path without anybody seeing, then it was a straight walk though the locks and down to the Proof House. There used to be an old house overhanging the locks. The old bugger inside would check my arse out from his bathroom window, but besides that there was never anyone around."

"The Proof House being the junction at Warwick Bar," I said, for the benefit of the tape, "connecting the Digbeth Branch Canal to the Grand Union Canal?"

The Bar was a narrow channel where the canals met and where, before they were joined, there had been several wharves and inlets to allow cargo to be transferred from one to the other. They're all bricked up now, with only the slightest hint of its past importance.

"I suppose," she shrugged. "It was always a bit lighter there. There's a lot of night work so the factory lights overspill onto the canal. Digbeth never had many street lights in those days, so it was easier to cut along the canal and get off at Great Barr Street."

"Taking you past the Rea culvert?"

"Yeah," she agreed, "but it was before then. At the junction itself. I was just about to turn left onto the Bar when I saw something straight ahead."

"Can you describe the junction to me?"

"Yeah. Before the junction it's just a bit of grass and ducks, then the canal widens out into a turning space. There's a direction sign telling the boats where's where, and behind that, on the other side of the canal, is the old Proof House. You can turn left past Warwick Bar and onto the Grand Union, while the branch carries on through an old tunnel under Fazeley Street and into the old Typhoo factory, but it's been fenced off, so you can't get in.

"Warwick Bar is a left turn parallel to Fazeley Street, so you either stay on the tow-path and follow it round, or you use a bridge to get to the road."

"And what did you do."

"I froze."

"Sorry?"

"He was right ahead of me, inside the tunnel, behind the fence."

"He?"

"I assume he. All I could see was a white anorak, or maybe a parka, I'm not sure. He was side on to me and I assumed he was a tagger, marking up the walls. That bit of the canal is always being sprayed."

"So if you thought he was a normal kid, why did you freeze?"

"I was just startled is all. I didn't usually see anyone, and you don't expect a kid to go tagging in a white anorak. I mean, I could see him from way back, plus he'd get it dirty pretty quickly, especially climbing around fences and using spray-paint."

"Then what?"

"I hoped he wouldn't notice me, so I walked as carefully as I could. He didn't seem to be looking my way."

"Apart from the spooky white anorak, what else made you think he was a ghost?"

"I didn't. Not then. It was after."

"After what?"

"I slipped under the tow-path bridge and the cattle walk."

"Cattle walk?"

"Yeah, its another older bridge that separates Warwick Bar from the Proof House, but isn't part of the canal. The council use it I think, but it's not a public walkway."

"So you turned onto the Grand Union Canal, and then what?"

"Then he whistled. To get my attention."

"What kind of a whistle?"

"You know," she said, pursing her lips and copying the sound. "The sort that calls you over."

"And then?"

"I turned. I couldn't see where he'd been standing any more, but then I saw him up on the cattle walk."

"On your side of the canal?"

"Yes. It couldn't have taken him more than a few seconds. There's no way he could have climbed around the fence, got on the tow-path, up on to the bridge and then get across the gap and fence that separated the tow-path bridge from the walkway. Especially without getting dirty or out of breath."

"And that's when you decided he was a ghost?"

Sandra nodded. "I was looking up at him. He was less than ten feet away and..."

"Yes?"

"His face wasn't... human. The anorak hood was pulled as tight as he could get it, but I'm telling you there was something else inside."

"A trick of the light, perhaps? Or the shadows?"

"That's the thing. There weren't any shadows. He was... well, it's like under those UV lights in a disco. His anorak was so white it was almost glowing."

"Almost?"

"Okay, it was glowing. Not like a street lamp that made everything bright around it though. It was just him. Totally white."

"What did you do?"

"I backed off a bit. I couldn't bring myself to scream; also, I might have weed myself."

"Did he say anything?"

"Not at first. Not until I turned and started to run. I was lucky I didn't have my heels on that night."

"Lucky? You didn't seriously wear heels to walk on the canal?"

"I can get a bit absent sometimes. But that night was crystal."

"So then what happened?"

"He said something as I ran away, but it was gibberish. I didn't stop to ask what he meant. I was halfway up the tow-path before I turned and looked back."

"He was still there?"

"Yes," she paused. "No. I mean, he'd vanished, but I could feel him. It was like he was standing behind me, breathing down my neck. Cold breath."

"Which way were you facing at this point?"

"I was looking back the way I had run, so he was in front of me I suppose, but my back was to him. I was scared to turn around."

"And did you?"

"Yes. I was telling myself it was my imagination, so I turned and started to walk. If he was there I was going to treat him like any pest and barge past him."

"And was he? There, I mean?"

"He said something as I turned around," she said, "but it was still gibberish." Her hands were shaking now, and she was more focused on keeping them steady than taking another drag from her half-smoked cigarette. "He was nose to nose with me as I walked straight into him."

Sandra stopped, bursting into tears with her last statement. I paused the tape to let her gather her thoughts before pressing on.

"Sorry," she said at last, returning to her fag. "This isn't like telling it in the bar. I'm stone cold sober and I'm not missing the borin' bits out."

"None of this is boring, I can assure you."

"Thanks," she smiled, her eyes smudging with tear-stained mascara as she did so. "It's good to get it off my chest."

"So you ran?"

"I just kept walking. Fast. In a straight line, 'til I got to Great Barr Street, then I was up the steps and onto the main road as fast as I could. I couldn't face cutting through the top of dirty end, so I took the longer way round, along the ring road. All the street lights and the cars made it feel a lot safer 'til I got home."

"And that was it?"

"Pretty much," Sandra nodded, drawing on her cigarette one final time before stubbing it into an ash-tray. "I quit a few days later because I didn't fancy using the canal any more, and since then I've always got jobs that could cover the taxi fare. It's a short hop, so it's not that much."

"And the ghost? Did you ever find anything else out?

"I asked around. There were a few stories, but nothing much."

"Stories? Like yours?"

"He'd been seen before, if that's what you mean. I forget who told me, but someone said it might have been the ghost of a gay *Doctor Who* fan that got stabbed at the culvert back in the eighties."

I smiled to myself. The old cliché of the gay Brummie Whovian wearing an anorak just never went away. More likely to be a teenage girl these days, but still, I made a note.

"Anything else?"

"A few taggers have died on the canals over the years," she said. "At least that's my dad's theory. His mates reckon it's some kid who died before he could finish his last tag."

"Your dad's mates? Was that just gossip, or are they local too?"

"Yeah, they're local. He used to drink down at *Hennessey's*. The old social club, on the High Street. Before it went posh. They know all the stuff that goes down in Digbeth."

***

Returning to my car, I stayed parked outside Sandra's block while I gathered my notes, and my thoughts. Digbeth is the oldest part of Birmingham, where even the bricks have memories, and any investigation could uncover... well, anything. Chase one ghost and you stumble across three more, each of them as mystifying as the first. I had to be methodical.

My first port of call was to the pubs of the area. At the time Sandra had seen the white anorak there'd been nearer thirty pubs in Digbeth, but now there were only eighteen or so. I say 'or so', because the number of pubs is defined by its boundaries, which are all different according to whom you speak. Digbeth is defined as the Irish Quarter by the Irish, Eastside by half the businesses, the Creative Quarter by the other half of the businesses. It includes Cheapside if you're a developer, Deritend if you're a clubber, and everywhere from Camp Hill to the Rotunda if you're looking to buy a new car. I stuck to the immediate vicinity of the canal and Fazeley Street. Small pubs with close-knit communities who were mostly workers in the area.

Eventually I tracked down a chap called Richard, who joined me for a fancy baguette in the bar of the *Old Crown*. He had sharp features and grizzled grey hair and, despite appearances, turned out to be a bit of a jack of all-trades. Ex-academic, environmentalist, council worker and, more importantly, a local. He'd spent most of his fifty eight years in and around Digbeth, as had his family before him. He'd lived there until the early sixties when, having been designated an industrial area, the few locals that were left started moving east into the suburbs. More importantly, at the cost of only a half of bitter, he was cheap to question and sober as a judge. He seemed to know pretty much all of the local gossip, and he agreed to listen to Sandra's tape with me and see if he could help.

Stepping out to my car, he sat in rapt silence as I slipped a C90 into the cassette slot and played back the interview. Having some interest in the area himself, he asked for a copy of my tape in return for his assistance. He then suggested I leave the car where it was and accompany him, there and then, down to the canal.

"I've not heard the *Doctor Who* fan thing," he said, guiding me from the *Old Crown*'s car park down and along Heath Mill Lane, "but the graffiti story makes sense. Up until the late 1980s the whole area was a graffiti magnet. Then we got some of the local kids in to do some volunteering along the canal. You know the sort of thing, tidying up and repainting. We actually encouraged proper street art instead of just graffiti, and for a while the kids we used took on the job of policing their artwork and making sure it was touched up."

Passing the Custard Factory and innumerable old warehouses and 'artist spaces', Richard finally brought me to a set of traffic lights and crossroads, pausing to tell me the story of the *Forge Tavern* on one side of the road, and the old Victorian toilet façade that had pride of place on the opposite side. Crossing over onto Great Barr Street, we slipped down onto the canal just as the road gave way to a hump-backed bridge.

It was late afternoon and early August, so the cool shade we found beneath the bridge and an even higher Railway viaduct was a welcome blessing. Here, Richard showed me some of the graffiti.

"It's a little patchier now than it used to be," he said, "but if you look closely you can see ghost tags under the paint."

"Ghost tags?" It was a new term for me.

"Taggers compete with each other by over-painting. If they have a grudge one will go to great lengths to paint over the tag of the other. With spray-paint there's usually no trace, but when you have several layers..."

I could see now what he meant. Faintly visible under the later paintwork were the names of former taggers, all but obliterated by the eighties project art, which was itself now obscured in places by more recent graffiti.

"The project kids grew up and moved on, I suppose," said Richard. "Makes it harder to protect their handiwork."

"I'd have expected a lot more graffiti over the years," I said, surprised that most of the original 'mural' was still visible.

"Tagging isn't about just filling empty spaces," said Richard. "It's about marking your territory. Usually they go for high points—the higher up the more dangerous it is, and therefore the better or more daring the tagger. Digbeth isn't that high, so the tag wars are more about danger than height. That's why you get the odd tagger death every now and then, which lends credence to the lady's story."

Leading me further along the tow-path, Thomas brought me to the Rea culvert, where he showed me the brick-based river, looking more like an artificial storm drain than the river that determined where Britain's second city was to be built.

"I'm not sure the cottaging happens much any more," said Richard. "Maybe at lunchtimes rather than on Saturday nights, but since they improved the lighting and opened up the Bond opposite—he pointed out a busy wharf and canteen on the other side of the canal—it's a bit more exposed."

The tow-path led us to Warwick Bar. There was a raised bench and a map of the waterways network on our side of the canal, and an old Banana Warehouse on the other. Ahead of us were the two bridges that Sandra had described—the cattle walk, and the arched bridge that formed part of the tow-path. Pausing to visualise the white anoraked watcher looking down from above, I followed my guide as he led me under the two bridges looping around and over the arched one, bringing us to the end of the tow-path. Here it split, with one branch leading up to the roadside and a recessed bench, while the right hand path led to the tunnel that ran under the road, stopping abruptly at the metal fence beyond which the anorak had first been seen.

"The Typhoo Wharf hasn't been used in years," said Richard, "and as I thought there is no tow-path beyond this point. The fence is just to stop people walking off the end late at night."

"So how could a tagger have been standing on the other side?" I asked.

"Unless he was already a ghost, I'm not sure it's possible."

Leaning up against the metal barrier, I pulled out my LED torch, shining it into the shadowy tunnel. Playing it across the walls I looked for signs of any graffiti or, as Richard had called them, ghost tags.

"See anything?" My guide asked.

I shook my head. The walls were pretty bare aside from the odd small scribble very close to the fence.

"I doesn't look too impressive," I said. "I mean, if a tagger was trying to build a reputation he'd want somewhere more visible, surely?"

"Let me see," said Richard, taking the torch and swapping places. As I had done, he played the light across the walls. Unlike me, he also shone it upwards.

"There," he said, the light playing on a large and, I cursed myself, unmissable ghost tag that spanned the entire underside of the bridge. The bricks looked as if the original paint had been cleaned away, leaving bare brick that was so much lighter than the brick surrounding it that most of the original tag still appeared to be legible.

"It's been scoured," said Richard. "Probably by *British Waterways*. The council use big sandblasters to clean the city subways, so I expect something similar was used. But I can't for the life of me work out why they'd bother."

Taking out my smart phone, I took as many pictures of the image as I could while Richard kept the torch steady. It was like playing Hangman, but after several minutes we'd worked it out. Switching to my contact list, I made a call.

"Hello, Sandra? We spoke earlier. The words you heard. The gibberish. Was it... *pulsanti operietur?*"

On the other end of the phone I heard a gasp, and then the line went dead. Cursing the foolhardiness of my approach, I assumed her response to be a yes.

"It's Latin," said Richard.

"Are you seriously suggesting that a teenage vandal wrote graffiti in Latin?"

"It's Masonic."

I looked Richard up and down. White. Middle aged. Middle class. Of course.

"What does it mean?"

"'To him who knocks it shall be opened'. When it's inscribed above a Lodge doorway the meaning is obvious."

"And here?"

"Cole was never a vandal," said Thomas. "He was an artist."

"Cole? That was his name?"

"It's a tagger's conceit. Names often have meaning. Cole is river a couple of miles to the east, which tells you that he came from that side of town."

"Nothing to suggest where or how he died though."

"Or if," said Richard. "I'm still alive."

He knocked on the metal fence three times, and everything changed. The world seemed to spin around me, and I thought back to our chat in the pub, and to the circumstances that brought me here. Had he put something in my food?

"What's going on," I asked, sinking to my knees.

"You knocked," he said, stretching his arms wide,"and the door is open."

As he spread his arms there was a glow, a halo that surrounded him, transformed him. The sun was low in the sky now, and he appeared to be different, white, like Sandra's ghost, but that was no anorak, and he was no spirit. The colour had drained from his face and his clothes, which now resembled a rumpled white coat. Reaching up to his forehead, he gripped something, just beneath his hairline. Drawing his hand down in a steady sweeping movement, he split his head from brow to neck, revealing what lay within.

"What are you?"

"I'm bound here," he said. "I have been for years. The city has its secrets, and I'm one of its guardians."

I looked around me. The world looked similar but... wilder, more overgrown, more decayed. It was as if twilight had come early, bringing with it something magical. Something surreal.

"Guardian of what?" I asked. "The old tea factory? The canal? The bridge?"

That's it. I thought. *The bridge*.

"You're not a ghost, you're... a troll."

"We were given such names once. Huldr. Tusser. *Brunnmigi*. Names that people fear because they don't understand. I crossed the great whale road with Bjarmr, the king who made this place his own. First I was bound to the sea-wood of his longship, then to his manor. As the mud of the Rea has claimed the past so I have become one with the fabric of his city. Its medieval builders enslaved me with their magic, but it has faded over time. Now words that once rendered me impotent have become the very tools that let me preserve and protect."

I should have found words like preserve and protect reassuring, but the look on Richard's— the creature's—face, was far from reassuring.

"Passers by telling ghost stories are good for me. They reinforce the magic. They feed me. But investigators..."

As he spoke I felt the tow-path beneath my feet give way, as if the very ground were swallowing me up. Too late, I realised that that was exactly what was happening. Brick as pliable as clay was grasping at my ankles, tugging me down into the ground beneath. I scrabbled for purchase as the sink-hole pulled me down and the last glimmer of daylight gave way to my former guide's bleached silhouette. Closing over me, I felt the earth slide until, moments later, I found myself settled in the air pocket where I now lie, starved of light and time, waiting until my own exhalations suffocate me. My last act was to pull my cassette recorder from my muddy, battered satchel. Setting it down before me, I pressed play/record, and told my final story.

THE VAMPIRE MOTORCYCLE

Today Digbeth has become a hub of activity, both relating to film, TV and other media. Shortly before the rise of the Custard Factory in the 1990s, it was a declining shell of dark, satanic streets and boarded up factories. The perfect location for a no-budget horror comedy that needed to use its Railway viaducts, large industrial buildings and the last few terraces of the area to create the impression of a dark, industrial suburb.

Filmed in Birmingham on the back of the *Central TV* Series *Boon*, in which many of the cast appeared, *I Bought a Vampire Motorcyle* was a tongue-in-cheek production made in 1990 and filmed in and around the Digbeth area. In the film, the vampire motorcycle—A Norton Commando —is possessed by a demon summoned during a biker gang turf war. Bought and renovated by bike enthusiast Noddy (Neil Morrissey), the bike is garaged by day, but by night comes to life to enact a series of grisly murders, investigated by garlic eating Inspector Cleaver (Michael Elphick), in its quest for blood.

Despite its clearly fictional and not-too-serious origins, the sounds of the vampire motorcycle can sometimes be heard racing down Fazeley Street in the dead of night as it roams the streets alone to satisfy its lust for blood. Of course, no bike can ever be seen, and no impaled corpses drained of blood have yet been found, but perhaps, one day, it will return for a sequel.

I Bought a Vampire Motorcycle © 1990, Dirk Productions Ltd.

ANDOVER STREET & BANBURY STREET

Just off Fazeley Street lies Andover Street, a short road that disappears beneath the railway arches towards Eastside. The original music studios used by UB40 once stood between the Digbeth Branch Canal and Andover Street. Demolished to make way for a new studio and housing development, plans were scuppered by its proximity to the Gun Barrel Proofing House. Birmingham thus lost a music studio, and gained a car park.

THE GUN BARREL PROOFING HOUSE

Beneath the railway arches of Digbeth lies a hidden cul-de-sac—Banbury Street—home of one of only two proofing houses in the whole of England. Until the late nineteenth century, most of Britain's gun's were manufactured in Birmingham, but with only one proofing house in the country, all gun barrels had to be sent to London for testing. Charles Pye's *A Description of Modern Birmingham* has this to say about the building:

"*Although government have at all times a large store of fire arms in the tower of London, yet, after the revolution had taken place in France, and England was threatened with an invasion, the numerous volunteers who offered their services at that time, to repel the enemy, required such a profusion to be distributed among them, that it became necessary to purchase large quantities from any part of the continent where they could be procured; and the volunteers of this town were supplied with muskets from Prussia. The words 'liberty' and 'equality', used by the French military, produced such an effect on the continent, that England was necessitated to manufacture arms for its own defence. Thus situated, application was made to the gun-makers in this town, but the number of hands at that time employed in the trade was so limited, that they could only supply small quantities; but when war was renewed, after the peace of Amiens, great encouragement being given by government, the manufacturers of arms in this town were, in the year 1804, enabled to supply five thousand stand of arms monthly.*

"*At that time, so many workmen had obtained a knowledge of the trade, that in the year 1809 the government were supplied with twenty thousand stand of arms monthly, and in 1810, the number was increased from twenty-eight to thirty thousand monthly; and that number was regularly supplied until the peace of Paris.*

"*In order to expedite the business, a proof house was established by government, in Lancaster-street, under an inspector from the board of ordnance.*

"An act of parliament was obtained in the year 1813, for the erection of a proof house in this town, where all barrels of guns, pistols, blunderbusses, etc. must be proved and marked, under a severe penalty; and since that time, the manufacturing of fowling pieces has increased to a considerable degree.

"It is situated on the banks of the canal, in Banbury-street, and is conducted under the direction of three wardens, who are annually made choice of from the body of guardians and trustees, they being nominated in the act of parliament. In addition to them, the Lords Lieutenants for the counties of Warwick, Worcester, and Stafford, the members serving in parliament for the said counties, for the time being, respectively, and the magistrates acting within seven miles of the town of Birmingham, are appointed as guardians."

Located within an enclosed courtyard, it was designed and built by John Horton, and now has Grade II Listed status but remains in use. This means that the occasional echo of gunfire can still be heard during daylight hours.

The Gun Barrel Proofing House, Banbury Street.

THE LOST ARMS

The licensing of arms-making became increasingly important in the wake of the Civil War, and during the years of Bonny Prince Charlie's Jacobite rebellion it is said that some of the Birmingham's gunmakers supported the Jacobite cause, stockpiling weapons in preparation for the pretender's march south into England. According to Walter Showell:

"It was believed that a quantity of arms were provided here by certain gentlemen favourable to the Pretender's cause in 1745, and that on the rebels failing to reach Birmingham, the said arms were buried on the premises of a certain manufacturer, who for the good of his health fled to Portugal. The fact of the weapons being hidden came to the knowledge of the Government some sixty years after, and a search for them was intended, but though the name of the manufacturer was found in the rare books of the period, and down to 1750, the site of his premises could not be ascertained, the street addresses not being inserted, only the quarter of the town, thus: 'T. S.—— Digbath quarter.' The swords, &c., have remained undiscovered to the present day."

THE EAGLE & TUN

Calling last orders for the last time in July 2009, *Ansells' Eagle & Tun* has been on death row ever since, silently watching as the landscape surrounding it changes, waiting for the looming arrival of the High Speed Rail link (HS2) to bring its walls crashing down.

Built by *James & Lister Lea* in the nineteenth century, its name was changed after the second world war to *The Cauliflower Ear* (a

The ghost of the Eagle & Tun sits on death row, awaiting the arrival of HS2.

name it shared with a nearby boxing club). It was known by this name when Birmingham band UB40 used it as their local. As well as writing a number of songs there (including *One in Ten*) the band used it as the location for their hit 1983 video for *Red, Red Wine*.

THE BULL'S RUN

No Birmingham walk can possibly be complete without at least one bovine anecdote. In March, 1877 the New Street terminus had a bull escape onto the tracks, running through the railway tunnel and out onto the Railway viaduct over Banbury Street. It leaped over the retaining wall and fell to its death on the street below where, Showell's *Dictionary of Birmingham* tells us, it was 'made into beef'.

NEW CANAL STREET & MERIDEN STREET

Late additions to the Digbeth landscape, New Canal Street and Meriden Street were laid out to cater for the railways and canals as they encroached upon the city, providing points of access to Albert Street, Moor Street, Fazeley Street and, of course, the Digbeth High Street. As the principal connection between 'old' Digbeth and the regenerated City Park and Eastside, it is an important route certain to remain when the HS2 Terminus is built alongside the Digbeth Railway viaduct that runs between City Park and Fazeley Street.

CURZON STREET STATION

The city's original London to Birmingham Railway Terminus was built in 1838 by Philip Hardwick, who designed the original—and almost identical—Euston Station Terminus. It now stands as the world's oldest surviving monumental railway structure, and is set to be incorporated into the entrance of a new high speed railway terminal.

In spite of its impressive pillared frontage, the growth of Birmingham was such that by 1854 trains were using the New Street terminus instead, and Curzon Street was relegated to being a goods station until its closure in 1966.

Inside, the three storey building has an impressive cantilevered stone staircase, as well as housing a bonded customs vault that runs from the basement down to the original platforms. A mummified cat, buried beneath the floorboards when the station was built, was discovered in the 1980s, and was displayed in a glass case set into the ground floor walls.

Curzon Street Station.

THE CURZON STREET HORROR

Birmingham has always pioneered new ideas, new technologies, and new forms of transport. As James Brogden reveals, not every discovery is the brainchild of an engineer...

The carpenter who nailed down the final floorboard hammered as loudly as possible in a vain attempt to drown out the miaows issuing from beneath. When he was done he collected his tools and turned to the circle of darkly-suited men watching.

"It's done," he said gruffly. There were tears on his cheeks, for, despite the roughness of his trade, he was a man with a love for all of God's creatures.

The man in the darkest suit merely held out a wallet, heavy with coin. Almost reluctantly, the carpenter accepted it.

Then he offered it back. "I beg you, sirs," he sniffed. "Let me..."

The darkest man's gloved hand closed with firm authority around the carpenter's fistful of money.

"Do not embarrass yourself any more than you have already," he said. "And do not speak of this." His hand tightened. "Ever."

The carpenter pulled away and fled, muttering "Monsters! Monsters, the lot of you!" while the cat's howls of agreement pursued him out into the midnight darkness of Curzon Street.

He glanced back and shuddered. In daylight he, like many of the others who had worked on its construction, had been impressed by the grandeur of the new Birmingham Station, with its four monumental granite columns giving it the impression of an ancient Greek temple; it had seemed a fitting gateway to welcome the brave new Age of Steam. Now, in the suffocating darkness of a midsummer night, it resembled nothing less than a giant mausoleum, rearing over the souls who passed the dread shadow of its threshold.

"Monsters, he calls us," mused the Chairman of the London-Birmingham Railway, as he locked the tall double doors. "Alas, progress is ever seen thus. Gentlemen, let us prepare."

The LBR Committee replaced their suits with long robes, and from boxes hidden in the customs cellar carried up items necessary for the ceremony: candles, a crate of Egyptian sand for marking out certain occult symbols, a translation of the ritual found inscribed on the walls of the great Temple of Bubastis, and a golden sistrum—a lyre-like instrument which the Chairman held in one hand as he consulted his pocket watch with the other. Finally, a box of mewling kittens was brought out. From within her place of entrapment, their mother, hearing the piteous noises, went into a frenzy of yowling and scratching.

Preparations made, the Chairman watched the second hand tick. At that precise moment, at the almost identical terminus building of the newly-constructed Euston station one hundred and seventeen miles away, an identical ritual was being readied with the other half of the litter and the kittens' father, who was similarly entombed. To create the mystical correspondences necessary to make the ritual a success, timing was imperative.

He looked up.

"Gentlemen," he said, "let us begin."

***

The carpenter's name was Samuel Mills, and he went straight to the *Fox and Grapes* on Park Road —a favourite haunt of navvies, railway yard workers and canal-boatmen—resolved that if he could not refuse the money then he could at least use a good portion of it to blot out the memory of how it had been earned.

Unfortunately for Mills, he was of that breed of drinkers who become garrulous long before insensible. More unfortunately, he picked a public house frequented by rail-yard watchmen employed by LBR, who were fiercely loyal to their paymasters and did not take at all well to hearing them described as devil-worshippers and petitioners of infernal powers.

Four of them followed Mills as he left the tavern to begin his intoxicated meanderings homeward, and caught up with him in a secluded spot by the Fazeley canal, where they proceeded to deliver a savage beating—the intention being to warn him off future slanderous accusations. The third and most decidedly unfortunate part of Mills' evening lay in the drunken exuberance with which they set about him, such that by the time they stepped back to examine their handiwork, Mills lay senseless with his face an unrecognisable and bloody mess.

Fearful of discovery, his assailants threw him into the canal to drown, and melted into the night.

***

Five weeks later, on a warm July night, the Committee reconvened at Birmingham Station to test the success of their undertaking.

This time they did not enter the building, instead assembling by its main entrance. A young cat, one of the litter belonging to the dead and now thoroughly mummified adult, was brought forth. About its neck was a collar, attached to which was a metal tube capped in gold at both ends. One end carried the coat of arms of the London-and-Birmingham Railway Company while the other was inscribed with hieroglyphs indicating the name of the goddess Bastet: protector, mother, guide. Inside the tube was a message, the details of which were known only to the Chairman and his counterpart, who was currently waiting by the main doors of the corresponding Euston Arch terminus.

The cat rubbed about his legs, purring as he took from his pocket a key whose design was a miniature of the sistrum which he had used to invoke the goddess' favour at their first meeting. It fitted the main keyhole perfectly, but had been created to open a very different kind of door.

Heavy tumblers rolled inside the mechanism.

He opened the door on a strip of absolute blackness wide enough only for a cat to slip through. A sudden draught issued from within; it was freezing cold and sharp with the dry perfume of ages-old incense and dust.

More than one member of the Committee took an involuntary step backward.

The cat inspected the gap for long moments in that particularly infuriating way felines have of remaining indecisive by doors, and then, with its tail high and proud, it stepped inside.

No sound or other disturbance issued from the blackness while they waited, until a faint miaow was heard from inside, and then out came trotting a similar, but obviously different cat—a brother or sister from the original litter. It too wore a collar with a gold-capped tube around its neck.

The Chairman bent to remove the tube, unrolled its contents and read them, and finally compared the message with one which had been couriered securely and secretly to him from his London counterpart several days earlier. With delight, he passed both to his colleagues.

"The procedure is a success!" he declared. "We have proven the viability of instantaneous transit between two remote but correspondent locations. Gentlemen, this is an historic occasion."

There was much fussing of the animal which had travelled so many miles in so few seconds and excited chatter and debate amongst the Committee members as talk turned to the future.

"The question remains," said one sceptic, "of how this can be developed on a mass commercial scale."

The Chairman dismissed this with a contemptuous flourish of his golden key. "When James Watt invented his steam engine, do you imagine he fretted over the details of creating a national railway system? No, that was for the men who came after him; he established the principle that it could be done. We still have years—decades, perhaps—of trial and experimentation ahead of us."

"Can we be sure that it will even work with people at all?" asked another.

"Obviously, yes, as it stands the transit space is likely to be most hostile to anything other than our feline friends, and so the first thing we will need to do is modify the consanguinity vector of the ritual to incorporate human blood, but we have ample resources to work with there. Think of the surplus population of our city's underclass. How many disappear every day without being missed?"

"Like myself, do you mean?" growled a new voice.

It was Samuel Mills, the carpenter.

***

Miraculous though it was that he lived, nevertheless he presented a frightful apparition. His clothes were tattered, while his face was still swollen and bruised from his beating, and he pointed a heavy pistol at the members of the Committee with grim determination.

"You thought to have killed me, you bastards, but I've been watching you for weeks. Now it's your turn."

"I'm sure I don't know who or what…" began the Chairman, and Mills shot him, quite simply and immediately. The pistol's report was shockingly loud. The Chairman fell against one of the columns, clutching his belly, his hand already a bright, glistening red. The rest of the Committee panicked and began to run.

"Hold your ground every whoreson one of you!" Mills bellowed. "Or I'll shoot you down like the pack of dogs you are!"

They froze.

Mills waved his gun at the station door, which was still ajar. "Get inside. We'll talk about this in there." He knew that the sound of the gun would quickly draw the local constables and believed that he could remain safe from them in the large stone building, at least until he could convince someone to investigate the truth of what he had discovered.

"You don't understand…" gasped the Chairman. "What's in there is…"

"Now!" roared Mills. He grabbed the wounded man and shoved him towards the portal.

Faced with the unknown ahead of them but certain death behind, the members of the Committee had no choice.

***

Their counterparts who were waiting by the huge bronze doors of Euston Arch for further messages from Birmingham shrank back in horror at the figures which shambled through without warning.

White-haired and naked, the travellers wept and shrieked with laughter as they clawed at their own eyes and dashed their heads against the stone pillars. One was already bleeding profusely from a severe injury to its abdomen, and they were all covered in innumerable claw and bite wounds, as if during their transit they had been savaged by wild animals.

In due course they were rounded up and delivered to Bethlem Royal Hospital for the Insane, where, since it was impossible to verify any of their identities, they lived out the rest of their mercifully short existences in anonymous and irretrievable madness.

The whole affair proved so disagreeable to those who witnessed it that the Bastet Project was quickly and quietly buried, and LBR got on with the more mundane but comparatively harmless business of rail travel. Euston Arch was subsequently demolished in 1961 despite strong objections going as far as Prime Minister Harold Macmillan. One campaigner later wrote: "Macmillan listened—or I suppose he listened. He sat without moving with his eyes apparently closed. He asked no questions; in fact he said nothing except that he would consider the matter." Nobody knew that during that conversation Macmillan's fingers were toying restlessly under the desk with a small metal tube capped with gold.

Twenty years later, a mummified cat was found by construction workers under the floor of what was by then called Curzon Street Station. Rumours that one of the carpenters had also discovered alongside it a small golden key and kept this for himself have never been substantiated.

THE WOODMAN

The Woodman undergoes redevelopment in preparation for the completion of City Park and the arrival of High Speed Rail.

Opposite Curzon Street Station, the *Woodman* public house stands alone, a solitary reminder of the densely populated area that, in the first half of the twentieth century, had come to be known as the Italian Quarter.

Built in 1896 by *James & Lister Lea* on the site of an earlier pub known as the *Thatched House* (c.1848), the *Woodman* survived because it was listed as the only example, complete with original features, of a pub of this particular red brick and terracotta design.

NEW BARTHOLOMEW STREET

All that remains of the first Birmingham Home for Lost and Starving Dogs alongside the second Birmingham Dogs' Home.

With the growth of the town's came a similar boost to its canine population. To curb this, Birmingham imposed a local dog tax in 1796.

This proved unpopular, and according to Showell:

"the fields and waters near the town were covered with the dead carcases of dogs destroyed by their owners to avoid payment of the tax."

The duty was repealed, but less than a century later, in 1867, dog licensing returned to the town. The use of dogs as 'beasts of burden' had been outlawed in 1854, and the popularity of Sunday dogfights with the local gangs—known as sloggers—required the police to have greater powers to deal with the problem. By 1885 Showell suggested that the problem of killing and abandoning dogs remained, stating that:

"It [The Rea] may be cleansed and become once more a limpid stream, if the sanitary authorities will but find some more convenient site as burial-place for unfortunate canines and felines."

It comes as no surprise that Sir Alfred Gooch gifted land in New Canal Street for the use of the Birmingham Home for Lost and Starving Dogs in 1892. In 1987 the dogs' home moved a few yards into a purpose built site in New Bartholomew Street. The sound of stray dogs yapping at all hours of the day and night has entered into the background sound-scape of the area, along with the metal-bashing, the trains, and the live music.

As of 2014, after 120 years in Digbeth, the dogs home will relocate to the village of Catherine de Barnes, close to the *Birmingham International Airport*.

THE MASSHOUSE & ST. BARTHOLOMEWS

King James II, Catholic monarch and sponsor of the Masshouse Chapel alongside St Bartholomew's Chapel.

At the top end of New Bartholomew Street, where it converged with Albert Street, sat the Birmingham Masshouse, an impressive Catholic Church and adjacent Franciscan monastery was built in 1687 and 1688 respectively. Within a few months, the Catholic King King James II (who had personally paid £125 for some of the church timbers) had been ousted by the Glorious Revolution. The largely protestant population of Birmingham, in defiance of the 1649 Act of Tolerance (which allowed non-Anglican faiths to worship openly), celebrated the King's departure by proceeding to tear the buildings down with their bare hands, burning what remained and selling off the stolen goods for use in housebuilding across the city.

Less than a century later, in 1749, St. Bartholomews, a grand neo-classical chapel, was erected to cater for a congregation of around 800. By 1847 it became a parish church that catered to the overspill from St. Martins in the Bullring. However, within a short space of time the encroachment of houses, the close proximity of the new railway lines and canals, the arrival of industrial warehouses, goods yards and, of course, the new dogs' home, precipitated a rapid decline in attendance by more and more of the city's well-to-do parishioners. A facelift and a further increase in capacity in 1893 failed to stop the decline until it finally closed in 1937. Struck by a German bomb in 1942, the structure fell into rapid decay until, by the 1960s, it was—ironically—swallowed up by a major new car park named after the Catholic church that preceded it, leaving only the haunted remnant of its graveyard behind.

The old St. Bartholomews graveyard

THE MARTYR TREE

It is perhaps ironic that as a pagan settlement, the early origins of old Birmingham are buried under layers of Christian history. Its concrete jungle had pushed back the memory that Mercia was the last heathen kingdom, and by 2000 any Brummie looking to celebrate the old Mayday traditions would need to have travelled into Shropshire, or Herefordshire, or Derbyshire to find the nearest festival.

But the roots of the old ways are growing in the ruins of its divided history. Among the graves once claimed by St. Bartholomews there is a tree that bears the shape of a man, a martyr perhaps, reminiscent of the god who first held sway over the Mercian kingdom. While the etymology of local place names confirms that heathen sons of Woden settled between Tamworth and Wolverhampton, it is the emergence of new roots that may yet reclaim some of that heritage. The green man has returned the the city and the Staffordshire Hoard has emerged from the soil of nearby Hammerwich. Meanwhile Beorma—almost certainly a follower of Woden—is making no little mark of his own, appearing as the namesake of bars and beers, new Morris dancing troups and even building developments. Perhaps the

old god's followers are right, and the appearance of the martyr tree is a symbol of his return, not as a hanged man, perhaps, but as a watcher over one of his ancient homes.

This connection has almost certainly resonated throughout Birmingham's history. Wayland, the old English smith seems have been well matched with the forges of Birmingham, and even as late as 1818 Charles Pye recounted the following poem, known only as *Birmingham, a fragment*, which he described as 'part of a prophetic oracle, delivered by the priests of the god Woden', in his *A Description of Modern Birmingham:*

> "Had we, Oh Birmingham, for thee design'd
> A trade that's partial, and a sphere confin'd,
> Thou'dst been a city, near some stream or shore,
> To bless some single district and no more;
> But thou must minister to thousand wants,
> Of cities, countries, islands, continents:
> Hence central be thy station—thus thy town,
> Must make each port around the coast her own.
>
> Let bright invention rove where no one awes,
> Unfetter'd by dull, narrow, civic laws,
> Which shut out commerce, ingenuity.
> Where bloated pride, in sullen majesty,
> And drowsy pomp sits notionally great,
> While she on every stranger shuts her gate.
>
> Let ingenuity here keep her seat,
> For works minute, or works immensely great,
> We to thy native sons the gift impart,
> Of bright invention, and of matchless art,
> Skill'd to devise, to reason, to compute,
> Quick to suggest, and prompt to execute;
> What some have but conceiv'd, do thou amend,
> Mature and perfect, to some noble end.
>
> Let fertile genius' bright, inventive powers,
> In all their vigorous energy be yours.
>
> Let savage nations who thy stores behold,
> Give Britain in return, their useless gold,
> Their gems, their pearls, their diamonds impart,
> And boast the change, and prize the gift of art.
>
> Thus shall thy polish'd wares of choicer worth,
> Gain all that's rare, from ev'ry clime on earth.
>
> Thy skill superior let our monarchs own,
> And deem thee a bright jewel in their crown."

ALLISON STREET

Once a densely populated street filled with working class homes and tiny public houses, the street, bisected by the Digbeth Railway viaduct as it passes into Moor Street Station, was once home to the notorious Allison Street gang, which was active in the area as far back as the Chartist riots of 1839.

BIRMINGHAM FRIENDS OF THE EARTH

On 1st April 1977 an old abandoned and unloved warehouse in the shade of the Allison Street Railway arch passed into the hands of the newly-formed *Birmingham Friends of the Earth*, whose volunteers, over the next thirty years, transformed the site into a small patch of green at the heart of brick-built Digbeth. The site is now a recognised eco-hub that includes low energy demonstrators, a cycle-repair and recycling workshop and a vegetarian restaurant.

The Birmingham Friends of the Earth buildings.

THE UMBRELLA WORKS

One old Digbeth factory restored to life is the Brolly Works, a Gothic-style three-storey umbrella factory and courtyard built in 1872. Since then it has been a clothing manufacturer and a crisp factory. With the decline of industry in the area, the factory gained a surprising and controversial new lease of life in 2007/8, when it was transformed into luxury inner city apartments, practically doubling the number of Digbeth residences in one fell swoop.

The Brolly Works.

2009 concept ideas for a statue of Beorma, founder of Birmingham, by Toin Adams.

2009 concept ideas for a statue of Beorma, founder of Birmingham, by Toin Adams.

THE BOX OF DREAMS

Storytelling is an important part of Birmingham's culture, and with a founder whose entire life story is a complete mystery, that should give the city's writers every opportunity to create a home-grown legend with a rich back-story. Heroes, monsters, creatures of myth—Beorma's homestead has so much history from which legends could be made.

Digbeth, 1906

Hilary and Ron had decided to get in one more wade along the Rea before the winter came. They had travelled a little further than usual, out of Edgbaston and onto the tow-path of the Grand Union Canal, following its bend through the Aston Locks onto the Digbeth Branch Canal. This brought them, eventually, to the Proof House Junction. They could have taken a more direct route, along Broad Street, onto New Street and then down Digbeth High Street, but water and the relatively dry dirt and cobbles of the tow-paths were preferable to the dust and mud churned up along Broad Street or one of the city's other main roads.

Now, just yards from the busy canal-side where ice, tea, bananas and the other fruits of the Empire were being unloaded to serve the country's fastest-growing city, the brothers unclipped their stiff white shirt collars and stripped away their dark school tunics, tying them together in a bundle which they carefully hid beneath some shrubbery. Easing themselves down into the lost river, they pushed their way past the thorns and nettles that overhung this part of the Rea. Around them, the familiar sounds of local industry were overwhelming, despite being dampened by the dense vegetation.

It wasn't really lost. The river was just too shallow to be navigated by boat, and as such had been siphoned off into the nearby pools that powered the forge and steam mills of Birmingham. While the rumble of distant trains and the creaking of nearby booms and winches could be heard in the background, it was the sharp, repetitive clang of the forge hammers beating against hot steel that resonated most in their ears.

Shoes and socks in hand, the boys made their way, ankle-deep, along the culvert. The acrid tang of freshly quenched metal caught in the back of their throats.

"Not far now, Hil," said Ron, the older of the boys, "it's just under the bridge."

"Are you sure?" Hilary asked, "it's dark down there."

Most of the river passed beneath the streets and foundries of Digbeth, and it was here that Ron had claimed to have found the mystery cave, sealed off by a rusty grill that had never been properly fixed.

"Here," he said, indicating a recess that was half swallowed by the shadows. Tucking his socks away and stringing his shoes together before slinging them around his neck, Ron reached forward to tug at the grate.

"It's a little stiff but..." he pulled with all his strength, and the heavy grate swung out towards him. "There. Come on."

Hilary glanced briefly around, to be sure they weren't being watched. It was unlikely, given that all the industry was happening overhead, and that this part of the Rea had no paths for folk to walk along, but it was still a little scary. A part of him was more worried about the troll that Ron had teased him about before they came.

"Come on, scaredy cat," Ron urged again as he disappeared into the recess.

Hilary swallowed. Trolls preferred mountains, and they hated big towns. But he was still a little afraid of the dark. Following in his brother's footsteps, he passed through the recess and into the cave.

It wasn't a spectacular cave, but since neither of them had been inside one before it was like stepping into another world. Adrenaline pumped through Hilary's veins as he let his eyes adjust to the poor light. Ron had already disappeared into the darkness, but the sides of the passage were close enough that Hil's fingertips guided him along. Wherever they were going he could feel the rush of air blowing gently against his skin.

"Hang on, Ron," he urged, trying to catch his brother up. He could only gauge the distance between them by the splish-splash of his brother's footsteps. "Don't go too far..."

"It's okay Hil," said Ron. "If we can feel the air then it goes somewhere."

"I wonder what it's for?"

"There used to be an underground fork leading off towards the old manor." Ron explained. "I think this is what's left of it."

Ron sounded closer now, as if he had stopped. Hilary reached forwards tentatively, and could feel the wool of his brother's tank top.

"What's wrong?"

There was a sharp scratching noise and the glow of light around his brother's head and shoulders as he struck a match against the surface of the wall. The smell of phosphorous filled Hilary's nostrils. Over Ron's shoulder he could see the flickering image of a wall. Before the light went out he could see that it started about three feet from the waterline. Between the wall and the water was a crudely shaped hole

"Shall we?" Said Ron, striking a second match. He was already kneeling down to duck under the arch. Crouching, Hilary peered into the hole before the light petered out. He was excited by what he saw, but also petrified. They must have been some twenty or thirty feet away from the river by now, and as they had moved forwards the air around them had got colder and colder. Even the tepid water around his toes was beginning to bite with the cold.

"Come on, Ron. We've gone far enough. Let's head back."

The sound of a third match was Ron's only reply as he disappeared through the hole into the tight passage that lay beyond. Hil thought about the troll. Then he thought about what Ron might be afraid of.

"There must be spiders down here," he said, playing on his big brother's fears. "Massive great spiders."

"You sod," said Ron, splish-splashing further down the crawl space as he picked up the pace. Hil could hear him strike another match. Clearly he too was scared, but the taunt had just urged him forwards.

The passage had opened up a little by now, and the flow of air had picked up enough to make any further matches useless. Moments later Ron whooped with joy as he emerged into an open space. Hilary followed, and found himself able to stand again. The air was calmer now, and the room resonated with a low, eerie clattering sound.

"It's the traffic up above," said Ron as if reading Hil's mind, "making the rocks in here vibrate."

"Smells bad," said Hilary, "like something died."

"And burned," added Ron, striking another match.

Ron was right. The small part of the cave that was illuminated was filled, amongst other debris, with charred and rotted wood. As the match sputtered Ron reached for the driest and longest piece of timber that came to hand, and set about trying to set fire to it with three or four more matches. The flame eventually took, and the wood started to snap and crackle, its brighter flame forcing back the darkness to show the cavern in all of its glory.

The first thing they noticed was that it wasn't a cave at all. The brickwork and the old wooden beams that held it all in place revealed them to be in a small pocket beneath the foundations of a building up above. An old cellar.

Kicking the wood and debris aside, Hilary picked up a piece of wood for himself, and gestured for some of Ron's fire. With the faggots lit, the boys stepped from the water and onto the rubble, circling each other as they looked around the room for anything of interest.

"Look," Hil gestured towards a distant corner, "what's that?"

Rising three or four feet from the rubble was what appeared to be a blackened stone object. It looked more like an above-ground tomb, the sort you found in a cemetery.

"It's a sarcophagus."

Scrambling over to the bier, the boys realised they were climbing on scattered boulders rather than debris. It looked like the sarcophagus had once been buried beneath a cairn of boulders. Ron brushed his free hand over the stone. His fingers came away black with soot. Up close the boys could see that the soot was hiding something lightly carved upon its surface.

"It's writing," said Hilary, excitedly.

"*Old* writing," Ron added, sharing his brother's excitement. Rubbing his shirt sleeve recklessly over the dirty stone, he exposed some more of the inscription. It wasn't latin or any other language he was yet aware of. The letters were stark and angular, with no curves. "*Really* old."

"Can we open it?" Hil asked, moving around to the opposite side of the bier. "Are we strong enough?"

"I don't know," said Ron, worried that something this old shouldn't be touched by someone who didn't know what they were doing. Then he thought about some of the damage done to Egypt and Rome in the name of archaeology. He and Hilary couldn't do any worse. "Let's give it a go shall we?"

Resting his fiery torch at the foot of the sarcophagus, Ron turned his attention to the stone lid. At fourteen, he was quite wiry, and Hil, two years his junior, wasn't much weaker. Between them he was sure they could shift it.

"Slide it downwards, to the bottom end," he said, taking a firm grip of the lid.

Hilary did likewise, and on the count of three they pulled back together. It was a struggle, with fingers slipping on a couple of occasions, and sweat breaking out as they exerted themselves again and again. Slowly but surely the slab shifted, its grating sound marking off their progress. Inch by inch the lid shifted until, pausing from the effort, Ron decided to peer inside the faint crack of the casket to see what might be inside. Picking up his burning faggot, he held it above the small gap that had appeared at the head of the bier. Moving it from side to side he tried to make out the shapes within as they reflected the light. There was a glint of metal.

"It's a knight!" Hil, who was also staring into the hole, was really excited now. "Buried in his armour."

"No," Ron shook his head. "Its too old to be a knight. A Roman, maybe?"

Ditching their torches again, the boys returned to the task at hand. Heaving away, they gradually exposed the mouldering body that lay within, shifting the stone lid closer and closer towards its tipping point. Oblivious to the risk, the brothers kept heaving until, inevitably, the slab shifted and the top half swung upwards as the weight of the bottom half crashed to the ground with a loud crack. Both Ron and Hilary had avoided being hit by the swinging slab, and they quickly found themselves staring at the broken lid, a mixture of guilt over the damage, and relief that their efforts had been rewarded.

Recovering their torches, the boys raised them up so they could see inside the sarcophagus. Ron recoiled at the spider webs that enveloped the body, while Hilary reached down and scooped away the offending threads to give them a better view of the man that lay beneath.

Somehow Hil had expected a dead body to be thin and skeletal, its armour loosely framing whatever remained inside. But this body wasn't like that at all. It had been a big man, easily six feet tall or more, and the body inside still filled out all the pieces of metal and fur and leather wrapped around it. In fact... Hil gasped.

"How can he be so well-preserved?" Ron asked, looking down at the warrior's face. Beneath a finely wrought metal helm engraved with men that seemed to be wrestling various animals—deer, bulls, boars and serpents—he could see the closed eyes that rested beneath the nose and cheek guards. Not sunken, but full as if the eyes beneath were still intact. Blowing away the thick layer of dust that covered the man's skin, he could see that it was grey and mottled, showing signs of age. Not old age, but middle age, like a man in his forties or fifties. The salt and pepper beard still looked well groomed, with beads and shiny jewellery braided into its white tips.

The mailed body was mostly obscured by the large sword and red leather shield that rested across his chest. While none of these items appeared heavily rusted or worn away, the shield had clearly seen some action, with a dented boss, notched edges, and several layers of chipped paint, the uppermost of which depicted the golden face of a beautiful woman whose eyes were black, as if shrouded by darkness.

Hilary reached forward, daring to lift the shield clear of the body. There was little resistance, just a light creaking sound as whatever held it in place gave way. Holding it up, he admired it by the light of Ron's torch. From the other side, his brother could see that the reverse of the shield had some crudely painted words on it, but any further investigation was delayed by what lay beneath the shield.

The warrior's mailed hands clasped not his sword, but a large, hefty book. Through this the blade of the sword was held in place like a giant bookmark. It was a large and finely wrought weapon with barely a hint of corrosion or discolouration, but compared to the book...

It was the size of a large bible, the sort that might rest upon the altar of a church, but it was made from ornately worked red leather that was embossed with golden metalwork inlaid with red garnets, like something a bishop or a king might have owned.

"Is it King Arthur?" Hil asked.

"In Birmingham?" Ron laughed, nervously. "Unlikely, although you never know. He does *look* like a King."

"I was thinking it because he looks asleep," said Hil. "Touch him, Ron. Touch him."

Ron looked down at the body. While it did look more like a sleeping man than a corpse, it was clear that he had been buried, and besides the shield, the sword and the book, other grave goods had been carefully placed around the body. There was an intricately carved casket of bone or bleached wood—it was too hard to tell in this light—carefully placed between the feet. There were also a ceramic jug, a drinking horn and other objects too obscure to identify.

Reaching forward to touch the body, Ron remembered the spiders, and paused.

"We shouldn't, Hil," he said, "I feel like a grave robber. What would Father Morgan say?"

"I'll do it then," said Hilary, reaching forwards and placing his hand firmly on the dead warrior's shoulder. He rocked it slightly, just enough to dislodge the book from the sword. Ron instinctively leaned forwards to stop the book from slipping away. As his fingers closed around the thick, heavy binding, something happened. There was a faint sound, like cracking glass, and a dark inky stain appeared at the point of contact and started to spread. Not just over the book, but over everything. Like an oily bubble the stain expanded outwards, creeping along Ron's fingers and enveloping his hand. Spreading across the warrior's body and beyond, sweeping over the sarcophagus, and over Hilary. The temperature dropped as he felt it wash over him and then, as the wave passed, the flame guttered for a moment; and the creeping stain was gone.

Ron looked at his hands. They were clean. The book he still clutched tightly bore no mark. Nor did the mailed fingers that now closed firmly around his wrist.

***

Oxford, 1940

With a scream, Ronald Tolkien sat bolt upright.

It was a recurring dream, as vivid as it had been when their silent screams had held them fixed in place all those years ago, unable to move as the mailed king rose up and towered, wordlessly, above them.

It had been real, he was sure. Hil had similarly vague memories, which they agreed were as if they had been seen through a fog, but the ancient warrior had been as vibrant and alive as any man. His fixed stare, hooded by the intricately decorated helm that glinted in the dim light of the chamber, the questions in a tongue that neither boy had heard before. They had long since agreed not to speak of the incident, but Ronald could never put it far from his mind. Glancing across the bed he could see that Edith—his beloved Lúthien—slept fitfully.

Carefully, he slipped back the bedsheets, easing himself into his slippers before crossing their room to the mahogany desk on which an old battered whalebone casket rested.

The one from his dreams.

The images on the box—not dissimilar to those he had closely examined on the Frank's casket—told of the voyage of a king across the great whale road. A king and his sons, one of whom, he was sure, had been his warrior by the river.

Beorma.

Lifting the lid, Ronald looked at what lay inside. The proof that his dreams were—must have been—real. The large red leather-bound book filled the cavity. As it had been before he prised it from the warrior's grip, it was weathered by time: not by the centuries, as it had been when he and Hil had found it, but by thirty years of dedicated study and translation. His very own philosopher's stone.

Prising it gingerly out of the casket, Ronald laid it down upon the desk and carefully let it fall open. As he did so a loose leaf —trimmed foolscap courtesy of King Edwards'—slid free. He bent and retrieved it, poring over the black ink which, he knew, was in his own hand.

Words written as a schoolboy but long since forgotten. He had no memory of translating the book, and yet, as one of England's foremost scholars in the matter, he could now read the flawless translation and hear, as he read, the voice of the king himself, reciting out loud words that the young monk who buried him had put to paper. The monk had been unaware that the king might rise, or that these words might themselves be lost when the falling of the Mercian axe was silenced by the ascension of Alfred.

Ronald sighed as he contemplated the treasure that rested in his hands. The tragedy of Mercia—the borderland—was that it had long been swamped by the corrupt histories of its jealous neighbours. History had recorded little of the deeds of Mercian Kings. Penda and Offa, perhaps, were remembered, but only in accounts that painted them as overlords of the most savage and rebellious of all the Anglo-Saxon Kingdoms. Of their kinsmen, before and after, little was recorded. Its champions were run ragged over the centuries, fighting hard against foes whose envy of the greatest kingdom ensured that all records of its great successes were erased, and that the nobility of its kings was subverted.

Mercia, proudly pagan, survived longer than the others of the heptarchy. They had fallen one by one and then, a century before the ascension of Offa, Christianity finally claimed it. As internecine politics threatened to tear the kingdom apart, the keeping of records passed into the hands of Diuma, the first Bishop of Mercia. His plans to rewrite Mercia's history with a Christian slant were confounded when Offa moved the Mercian capital from Tamworth to Repton. Many writings were lost, and within the year the Northmen had come from Haerethaland, and history took second place to survival as the Saxons and the Angles were forced to turn their attention towards the savage Vikings.

Ronald knew the story so well and yet he couldn't share it. Not as a respected scholar. The book appeared to be too new, too recent; like a modern forgery. No serious scholar would believe the tale of its discovery, and yet every fact that he had checked, every fragment he had examined, from Bede to Beowulf, had corroborated what he called the *Beormassaga*.

"Mercia was the youngest of the kingdoms, forged by the sons of Icel. A hundred years had passed since the first of the angles and the Saxons came to claim the empty throne of the English bear, displaced by the Huns and forced to make new homes in the fertile isles of chalk and tin. But the Anglian Icelings came from more northern climes, bringing

with them a hardier temperament and a desire for action. They settled first on the eastern coast and then, when they set to squabbles among themselves, they forged a new inland kingdom where the foreigners lived.

"These Icelings did not travel alone, and among their kith were the last of the Beorm, a northern tribe of walrus ivory and sable-fur traders from the lowland seas of the cold north-east far beyond the kingdoms of the western coast. Chief among these was Beorm, whose fish and fur-rich territory was coveted by the tribes of the Rus and the Hun, who mounted raid upon raid against his tribe, killing many of its women and children, dividing the kingdom and depleting its numbers before forcing them to seek refuge among the Wes and the Geats.

"Beorm, the last chieftain of his tribe, took up the call to cross the north sea and give support to the Icelings in return for a great many riches that were never forthcoming. Dissatisfied, he made plans to return east and to lead the fight back against the Honings. Instead, the Iceling chieftain Creoda offered him a deal, to strike west and share a new kingdom with him, on the fringes of the Anglian territories.

"An oath was sworn, and the families of Creoda and Beorm set upon a hill the fortress of Tamworth, overlooking the waters of the Tame and the Anker. From here the land of Mercia was quickly settled.

"To the east, jealousy among the other Icelings grew, for the lush valley of the Tame and the great Arden wood that lay beyond were very fertile, but none dared stand against Creoda or the mighty Beorm, whose great axe was feared in all the Saxon kingdoms. This great reputation was further enhanced by the tales of Beorm's excursions beyond the border, where even the foreigners were wary of his temper. For this reason they waited on Beorm's demise, but that of Creoda came first, and Pybba ascended the Mercian throne.

"Honoring his father's oath, Pybba kept only the north of the borderland, and Beorm set forth to carve his own territory further inland. In his absence, however, the court of the king was riven by family feuds, for Pybba had more than a dozen sons and daughters, each of whom coveted the throne. Whatever treachery ensued, it was a bloody night that saw Pybba and his heirs slaughtered and Cearl, backed by Raedwald of the Eastern Angles, seize the kingship.

"Days later, Beorm heard the news, returning with his men-at-arms to confront the usurper, who held his own sons—Beorma, the eldest, and Breme, who was just a baby—and those of Pybba, the eldest of whom were Penda and Eawa.

"Cearl's fear of Beorm was great, and a compromise was struck:

the children would be freed in return for Beorm's surrender. Afraid for their lives, the great chieftain agreed, surrendering alone and instructing his men-at-arms to spirit the children away to the land of the Geats he had once called home.

"With the children released, Beorm strode towards the king's fort, unarmed and with his arms held wide as a sign of his good faith. Cearl, still fearful of the chieftain's anger, ordered him cut down by spears only twenty paces from the fort. Impaled, the furious chieftain stormed the gates, forcing them open with his bare hands until, as he sank to his knees, Cearl himself arrived to strike the head from his shoulders.

"On that night a second oath was made as Beorma, Penda and Eawa swore upon the blood of their fathers, even as the men-at-arms bore them north to the place of caves, where a flat ship of twelve benches waited to carry them back across the northern sea..."

***

Ronald paused, closing the book. He knew the rest of the story; of how Penda and Beorma would return to reclaim the kingdom; of how Beorma stood aside while Penda reigned; of how Beorma tried and failed to live as a brewer of beer and a farmer of bees, reclaiming the crown to rule Mercia for only two days. He was forgotten as a king perhaps, but his sons—the bastard and his legitimate heirs—still managed to shape the future. First of Mercia, then England, and then...

Ronald looked at the book that lay beside the box of dreams. *The Concise Oxford Dictionary of English Place-Names*, ed. E. K. Ekwall. It was the latest edition, a gift from his good friend Eilert, sent not with a note but with a bookmark. Opening the book to the indicated page, Ron read the entry underlined, and smiled.

"Birmingham probably meant 'the Hamm of Beornmund's people' (OE Beornmund-ingaham). Or the direct base may be a pet-form Beorma from Beornmund."

Not quite what he'd argued, but close enough. For now.

THE BEORMA QUARTER

Perhaps the most visible and controversial development in recent years have been plans to develop an ambitious new twenty story building known as the *Beorma Quarter*. Backed by Kuwaiti developers, the plan to build a glass 'city within a city' in the heart of Birmingham has been welcomed by the authorities, but met resistance from some local businesses.

Filling a site once occupied by several medieval burgage plots, the development covers the area that lies between *Selfridges* at the Bullring and Allison Street in Digbeth proper. This area includes an old Music Hall, the former *George Tavern*, a number of converted Victorian offices and shops, a listed cold store (used for keeping ice imported along the city's canals) and *Hennessey's* —one of Digbeth's many Irish taverns—whose courtyard was found to be the site of several medieval graves.

Cutting across so many sites of archaeological interest, including Birmingham's original artesian well (after which Well Lane was named), great care has been taken in making the building fit in with the surrounding area. The tower, built on a slope, will be as tall as the Rotunda but, sitting lower on the horizon, won't obscure it from the skyline. On the ground floor the development will maintain the shape of the original medieval plots; and even the artesian well is set to draw water from the Birmingham aquifer to both heat and cool the building, making it a major architectural feature intended to showcase what the developers are calling the gateway into Digbeth.

With plans for hotels, offices, apartments and incubation space, even the name draws on Birmingham's history. The first major move from the site was *Hennessey's*, who in early 2011 relocated to an empty warehouse and office on Allison Street, but have plans to open a bar on-site when the Beorma Quarter is complete.

DIGBETH HIGH STREET

Birmingham's High Street originally stretched from Dale End to the top end of the Digbeth causeway, which was originally known as Well Street. As the town expanded, the High Street joined the causeway, passing the Manor House and St. Martin's Church at the Bull Ring, and heading down into the Rea valley.

It is said that a castle was raised in 1140 within a bow-shot of St. Martin's, and that it was demolished a few years later, in 1176, by order of King Stephen. During the interim time Birmingham's Manor House was built (c.1154), and its Lord, Peter de Bermingham, was granted license by King Henry II to hold a market every Thursday at his castle.

While the walls may have fallen, the moat remained, and the town's markets became the most successful in all of England, being held under the shadow of the Moat House (as the Manor came to be known) until the eighteenth century.

Digbeth High Street, including Smithfield.

THE BIRMINGHAM GIANT

This fall of Birmingham's castle is remembered in local folklore, which says that once, long ago, there were two giants, each of whom lived in a castle upon a hill.

The Giant of Dudley was the lord of the Giant of Birmingham, but when the latter grew fat off the land he refused to serve his master any longer. The Giant of Dudley grew angry, and picked up a great stone which, as an act of war, he hurled from the top of his own hill all the way to that of Birmingham where, with terrible accuracy, the War Stone demolished the the castle and landed upon its Giant, killing him.

This legend perhaps reflects a more mundane story. Peter de Birmingham had been the Steward of lands owned by the Paganells, and when the latter openly rebelled against King Stephen in 1173, their lands were confiscated. Both the Dudley and Birmingham castles were demolished, and the 'the noble and warlike family of the Bremichams' were installed as lords of the manor.

Of course, the origin of giant stories goes back much further, although whether the tales of those in the Midlands are of English or Irish—or christian or pagan—origin will never be certain. Hubert d'Arbois, in *The Celts and Hellenes* (1897), suggested that England was once the home of 'an elementary big-boned tribe whose divinities were Gog and Magog', while '…the various races that have successively inhabited Ireland trace themselves back to [...] Magog or Gomer, son of Japhet.'

THE GIANT'S HEARTBEAT

In this next tale, Anne Nicholls gets to the heart of our fears and superstitions, reminding us why tall stories and bawdy tales are always the best starting point for myths, legend and modern urban fantasies.

"Amo, amas, I love a lass." Noll Weaver and his friend Baldy giggled at their daring. Normally Father Dodds was drunk and savage. Today he was drunk and asleep. Around him the hall of the Guild School rang to the chants of Latin conjugation, but seeing the empty tankard dangling from the master's hand, Noll and Baldy chortled. "Amas, amat, she had a cat."

Outside, the sun beat down, bringing the stink of tanneries and slops from the River Rea. Along the lane, Heath Mill clattered to the grinding of corn, and hammers rang on the anvils of Digbeth. Today was Noll's eleventh birthday, and he wished he was fowling on the marshes beyond Deritend instead of cooped up in a classroom. He began to carve his initials on his desk.

The door slammed open.

"Eh? What?" barked Old Doddery, and fell off his chair. He tried to get up but his stick tangled in his legs. The schoolboys smothered a snigger. That was the last time Noll would find anything funny for quite a while.

"Please, sir," said the frantic servant who'd burst in. "It's Master Weaver, sir."

Noll jumped up. "W-what's happened?"

"Yer dad's fell off his horse. The missus says you've to come at once."

"Oliver Weaver," yelled the priest. "Get back here and ask permission!" But Noll dodged the flailing cane and raced out the door.

***

All that was thirty years ago. Now Noll looked about the dim-lit taproom. King Henry had done away with the Guild of the Holy Cross. It hadn't made much difference to Noll. With his father's death his mother had been robbed of the business, and shortly after, of life itself. No more Latin for Noll. At the age of twelve he'd had to earn his daily bread, and not much of that for the first few years. Now the school was the *Old Crown* coaching inn and Noll was head ostler. Over his bread and cheese he supped his ale and listened out for the Warwick Flyer.

Late again. These autumn fogs were the devil's playground, and the smoke from the forges made it worse.

A stranger came in, dyed feathers nodding on his hat. He shoved arrogantly through the crowd, head high as though a bad smell were under his nose. Well-to-do, he was, by the look of his doublet with its slashed sleeves and the pomander in his hand. But the *Old Crown* was packed to the rafters. The only seat to be had was the one at Noll's table. In a strange accent that came hard to the ears, the foreigner said, "Mind if I join you, my good man." It wasn't a question. He was already settling his rump.

Noll shrugged. "Your funeral."

Raising his brows, the stranger swigged from a pewter tankard. He neglected to thank the serving-wench who'd brought it. "Your good health."

Noll's eyes narrowed at such rudeness to his Bess. "If it's good health you're after you didn't ought to go sitting in that seat. Nor drinking out of that there tankard."

"Whyever not?"

"Aah, I'll tell you the tale for a pint. Bargain," Noll added persuasively, seeing the man's sceptical expression. "I dain't reckon your life's worth less'n that but it's up to you."

***

"See that there chair?" Noll said, smacking his lips in appreciation of free ale. He'd squashed up on the bench to let the stranger—his name was Jack de Picadilly—in beside him. They faced the empty seat. "Belonged to Father Dodds, it did, back when this were the Guild-school. See his initials on the backrest?"

"So why shouldn't I sit in a cleric's seat?" Arrogant, he sounded. "He's got no use for it now, I take it."

"No more he has," agreed Noll. "Not now he's drownded. My mate Baldy—Theobald, he were, by rights—Baldy were the one who saw him go in the river. See, Baldy were a cooper and Doddery were his neighbour." Noll raised his pint and his elbow knocked Jack's, with the result that brown ale sloshed over the furriner's codpiece.

"What's that got to do with anything?" Angrily Jack swabbed at the front of his hose, much to the amusement of Bess the barmaid who mimed a rude gesture behind his back.

Noll hid his grin in his beer. "Hold your horses. I'm coming to that. You'd ha' known if you wasn't a furriner."

"Foreigner? I'm from London."

"S'what I said. They dain't talk proper down there. See, Baldy being a cooper, he had muscles on him, and being Baldy, he had a thirst on him too. He come in from his workshop one night. Raining pitchforks points down, it were, black as a chimbley-back, and the Rea roarin' in spate. Mind Baldy were powerful fond of his leg-shaker and the moment he got in out o' the rain he snatched up the first tankard he seen. Which were that 'un." Noll jerked his chin to indicate the shapely pewter in front of them, the very one Jack had insisted on.

"Knocked it straight back, he did. Then he goes, 'Aah!' and Father Dodds says, 'You young varmint! That were my ale!'

"'That were my firkin what you never paid me for. Last Michaelmas, it were, and you been promising me them two groats ever since.'

"Well, back and forth they went. No love lost between 'em you see, what with Baldy still deaf in one ear where Doddery knocked him off the bench when we was at school, and Dodds bein' a graspin' old drunkard what would cozen anything out of anybody and say it were for God. He turned Church of England the minute King Hal put the word out but he weren't no better as an Anglican than he had been as a son o' Rome. They near come to blows so the landlord chucked 'em out into the storm. Last thing I 'eard were Baldy shouting, 'Gimme back my firkin or you owes me two gallon o' brown ale.' Later, what with the millrace thunderin' loud as cavalry on a bridge, 'alf the taproom reckoned that weren't what Baldy said at all. Apparently they thought Dodds had said if Baldy touched his tankard again he'd be cussed with hell-fire and Baldy said Doddery were too mean to part wi' anything, not even a cuss.

"Well Baldy stopped to water the horses, as you might say, and Father Dodds staggered on beside the river, mumbling but none too brave now it were just him and Baldy splashing about in the dark. Baldy were just doin' up the drawstring of his hose when he heard this terrible noise. First he thought it were the giant—"

"What giant? You haven't said anything about a giant!"

"Gods' Wounds, Jack, are they all as hasty as you down London? I'm tellin' you, ain't I?" Noll quaffed some ale and wiped his mouth with the back of his hand. All the time Bess loitered, grinning at the twinkle in her light-o'-love's eye.

"See, back in the olden days Brummagem had this giant, and Dudley had another. Dudley's a village out beyond West Brom. The two on 'em was at war. They do say as how our giant lobbed this huge great rock at the Dudley one and he lobbed a bigger one back what done our old feller in. You can still see the War Stone out past the sand-pits if you don't believe me. Our giant had a son who weren't up to much. Not much bigger than a cottage, by all accounts. And Father Dodds were the one whose accounts we go by. Mind, he also said there was cockroaches swarmin' ower his cassock when he'd had a skinful, but he lived in a shanty hard by the millrace so who knows? Anyway, he weren't the only one who'd heard ghostly 'eartbeats comin' from up the valley. They do say as it were the little giant's shade whose 'eart beat fit to bust wi' remorse 'cause for years he were too scared to avenge his old dad.

"So just as Baldy laces 'is family jewels back in place, he hears this 'orrible thump comin' out o' the night. 'Must be the giant,' he says to hisself, 'cause what else could make a bang loud enough to drown out the roar o' the torrent?'

"Then a fork o' lightnin' splits the sky, lit the stream up bright as day. There's this whistling noise and Baldy sees something huge flyin' through the air to land slap dab on Father Dodds' shack. Then bits of shack go flyin' through the air and blast poor old Father Dodds right into the millrace. And that's the end of him."

By this time Noll and the stranger had both finished their ale. Each looked first at the other, then at the full tankard, and back again.

"Wait a minute!" exclaimed Jack. "If your cooper was the last one to drink out of that tankard, it's not cursed at all. You're having me on."

"Ah, see, that's where you go off bein' hasty again. Baldy staggers back in the taproom looking like a drowned rat only pale as a ghost, and plumped right into Father Dodds' chair. 'The giant only just missed me!' he says. 'Quick, Bess, gimme a drink in Doddery's tankard! I ought to been killed but he were instead. His cuss were my blessin'.'"

Bess leaned her generous bosom over the furriner's shoulder. "'S'right, sir. Baldy reckoned Father Dodds were that evil the cuss bounced right off the tankard and back at the old misery hisself."

From outside came the clop of hoofs and the rattle of harness as the Warwick Flyer finally turned into the yard. Hearing it, Bess touched the hem of her apron to her eyes and essayed a sob. 'I'll never forgive myself, sir. I filled that tankard and put it right in poor Baldy's hands. There was a bang! like Hell's gates slamming open. Our giant slaughtering the Dudley one, that were, but the shock made Baldy drop down dead where he sat. Nobody's touched that chair since. So don't you drink from that tankard, sir, nor sit in Doddery's seat. And don't worry, sir, our giant's heart bust when he lobbed that final rock that killed the one from Dudley, though sometimes you can still hear it beating all ghost-like from the best bedroom. Oh, that's the one you're in, ain't it? By the way, Missus says she's sent your supper up."

Bess stepped back and Jack stood up. Uncertainly he gazed at the tankard, and at the empty chair. He mithered a little, then tossed the price of a pint on the table and a penny for the barmaid. "Thank you kindly for the warning. I bid you good night."

Once he was safely up the stairs, Bess dropped into the empty seat. She laughed so hard her stomacher pinched.

"Reckon he dain't know the sound of a tilt-hammer, Bess?" grinned Noll.

Once she'd recovered, she gasped, "Oy, greedyguts, gi's a swig o' that ale."

Noll reached across and kissed her fingers. "For you, my beauty, anything. 'Ere, come and sit on my knee. Baldy's just come in. I've been savin' him a place.

"Hey, pal, where you been?"

Baldy Cooper hung his driving coat by the fire. "God blind me! The fog's thicker'n a shroud. Got chased by a highwayman and the axle bust. Thought we'd had it but Jerry driv 'im off. It's taken us all this while to get the coach fixed."

"Should ha' stuck to cooperin'."

"What, and risk that stupid cannon foundry blowin' the place up again? Not on your life. Good health!"

PARK STREET

The north of the Manor would have looked out upon the Little Park, which begins where Park Street is bisected by a Railway viaduct, spreading out over what is now Eastside to join the Lower Meadow Hill that preceded Fazeley Street. In time it grew to become the define the boundary between Digbeth and the rest of the city, being a popular choice for inner city car parks as well as pubs like the *Fox & Grapes* around which the Park Street Gang emerged to join the city's slogger scene, becoming the site of a major riot in which cutlasses were drawn against the city's Irish workforce *(see Appendix II: Law & Order)*.

THE BIRMINGHAM MARKETS

The gyratory that separates Digbeth from the city's many markets is known as Smithfield. This, and the site of the former Birmingham Manor, grew to form the most successful set of markets in all of England. Richard I confirmed the de Bermingham's market charter in 1189, and from that time they have continued to grow.

The Cattle Market, originally held on Digbeth High Street itself, was moved uphill to High Street, Dale End in 1769, and then to Deritend in 1776. A Pig market remained in New Street, but in 1817 the Smithfield Market was opened, consolidating the sale of horses, pigs, cattle, sheep, and farm produce. When plans to move the markets out of town to Duddeston were raised, an emergency anti-moving-the-cattle-market meeting was held, retaining the site until it moved, for a time, to Montague Street.

By the nineteenth century *Beardsworth's Repository for Horses and Carriages* lay to the southwest of Smithfield, allowing for bests of burden to be auctioned close to the livestock.

Despite the name, most of the modern Bull Ring site was taken up by the Corn and Vegetable Markets as a programme of demolition by the street commissioners followed. Over the years the sale of fish, hide, skins and wool were consolidated, overtaking the site of the old Manor and its moat.

The redevelopment of the markets and the new Bull Ring between 1961and 1964, along with the development of its 'concrete collar' and its new high-rise suburbs, earned Birmingham a reputation as a concrete jungle filled with brutalist architecture. Plans for its transformation into a newer, more pedestrian friendly Bullring began less than twenty years later, and by the turn of the millennium the work had begun.

JOHN A' DEAN

The Manor's moat was serviced by a small medieval drainage ditch which connected it to the Rea some forty yards short of the Deritend Bridge. According to Pye and Showell, the ditch was called John A' Dean's Hole after a labourer who fell into it and was killed, presumably during its construction.

DR. JEKYLL & MR. BIGFOOT

Everyone visits Birmingham at least once. The trick is that, no matter how short your stay may be, if you explore you'll make the most of it. Here Theresa Derwin tells us how, in April 1886, just three months after he wrote Strange Case of Dr Jekyll and Mr Hyde, Scottish author Robert Louis Stevenson did exactly that...

I dreamed of Hyde again last night.

The visit to *Smedley's Hydropathic* had been a foolish idea. The fatigue that I inevitably suffer, simply through the acts of travelling and working, gives me no respite. Fanny, as dutiful and attentive as a wife can be, has already learned to sleep deeply, so that when I wake she is oblivious to my torment. The air of Birmingham is humid and lies thick upon my chest, while our brief sojourn in Matlock had exhausted the supply of opiates with which I would usually endure the day.

The terror of the dream, in which the hands of my cocaine-fuelled creation, Edward Hyde closed hard around my neck as if to take his revenge against me for bringing him to life, segued into a particularly irritating coughing fit that roused me with a stifled scream. Sleep is no relief from pain, for I dream of it even as I endure it in my waking hours. With my throat raw and the tightness of my chest throbbing unbearably, I sat up, gasping, desperate to take in the air. Blindly, I reached for the glass of *vin mariani* I had set upon the bedside table earlier in the evening.

After the calm of Matlock, the rowdiness of England's fastest growing town had done little to help my slumber. The unfamiliar surroundings and an uncomfortable bed made me restless despite the pain. Forcing myself to rise, I shambled over to retrieve my clothes. My hands trembled in the half-light as I struggled to button up my favoured velveteen jacket before retrieving my walking stick and slipping from the room, leaving my sweet Fanny to lie undisturbed.

It was madness. Our hotel, the *Queens*, adjoined the New Street railway terminus in the aptly named Stephenson Street. Having an engineering pedigree of my own, I cannot help but be riled whenever I am asked what it is like to be the son or grandson of a great railway pioneer.

"I am Stevenson with a 'v'," I invariably respond rather grumpily. "Lighthouses and literature, not railways and bridges."

Stepping out into the night, the warm air felt as if the streets themselves had soaked up the sun's heat for their own selfish purpose; as if the gates to Hell lay just a few yards beneath my feet. Hell, of course, is exactly how many describe Birmingham. Even at night the smells of blood and offal, oil and fired metal filled my nostrils. I had chosen to make my way downhill, cutting through the empty markets where the smell of old meat obscured all else as I took it upon myself to pause at St. Martin's in the Bull Ring. Here, among the graves and the shadows of the high town, I found some brief solace, calming my nerves once more as I withdrew a small wooden case from my jacket. In it lay my last resort, a syringe filled with the concentrated cocaine tincture that I would usually reserve for writing binges—hence, I suspect, this present account.

Drawing back the sleeve of my jacket, my skin crawled as I exposed it to the air. Even in the moonlight I could perceive the rash that afflicted me like a dose of *Saint Anthony's Fire*, but I barely hesitated, plunging the needle into the first vein that I could find. It was a struggle, especially in the dark, but a second attempt filled me with blessed relief.

I sagged against the nearest headstone, my eyes half-closed as I let the mixture pump through my veins, some semblance of relief at last flowing through them. As the pain lessened and became almost bearable, I propped myself up, using my stick to stand and look beyond the church. Pushing forwards, I made my way onto Digbeth, the town's oldest street, which I understood led into a labyrinth of narrows and dark passageways much like those preferred by my literary nemesis. It was with Hyde's eyes that I looked down upon the causeway, venturing forth among the cobbles with an urge inside of me. It was the darkness I had felt many times before, the hunger for danger and for hedonistic distractions. But this wasn't London, nor Edinburgh, nor Bournemouth, nor any town I truly knew. Damned fool that I was, I left the offal stench behind me and headed deep into the labyrinthe that lay ahead.

How long I walked—or staggered—I could not be sure. All reason was left behind with Fanny in the *Queen's Hotel*, while here, deep in the dirty heart of a foreign town, I found something, someone, to help me through the night.

Her name was Maggie. Maggie McMahon. A doxie out late, fuelled by booze in her belly and no pennies in her purse. She was skinnier than I, and slighter, with a fresh face and wholesome teeth that belied her trade. Doubtless she was just a girl, but with her gin-fuelled mood she encouraged me, and I gave up any pretence of restraint, as if Hyde himself were unleashed upon her.

***

I was roused by fingers of moonlight that reached towards me through the holes of the tattered sheet that covered the window. Blinking, aching, I took in my surroundings. It was a bare room but for three mattresses, all occupied by shapeless lumps I could not quite identify. Except the one I found myself sharing with Maggie McMahon. As she lay cradled in my arms, I looked down upon the bruises applied by our passion, and I realised that the darkness had indeed provided a relief with which no drug could compare.

I disentangled myself, drawing the curtain aside to compose my attire before sneaking from the tightly packed house into a shared courtyard. They were back-to-backs, with probably two dozen sharing the communal space.

"And where might ye' be headin'?" Called a Celtic voice from the shadows.

Startled, I turned to look and there before me was a young lad of around sixteen years, wearing a rumpled green suit and waistcoat, with a silk scarf and a tilted cap.

"I'm sorry," I said, uncertain of how to respond. "I need to go—"

"Has 'e paid ye' luv?" The boy called over my shoulder. Turning, I saw that Maggie was stood behind me, adjusting her clothes and looking back towards him. Up close I could see they were alike. Brother and sister, perhaps.

"'E just had tuppence on 'im," she said by way of explanation. I'd been lucky to have that, for this wasn't a planned assignation.

"Look," I said, suddenly fearful of where this might go, "I can get more—"

"I'm sure ye' can," said the boy, But that would'na look so good, lettin' ye out on trust. Better just tae punish ye' and let ye' on yer way."

Punish? I wasn't sure what he meant, but he left no time for speculation, calling out to a friend from the shadows. As I watched, it seemed as if the shadows themselves were stepping into the courtyard, for whoever he was, he filled the whole space of the archway leading into the courtyard from the street beyond.

In that moment I felt that I had come face to face with my nemesis. He towered above me, around seven feet or more in height. His poorly tailored suit was stretched and worn, exposing a great swath of muscle and sinew around his neck, forearms and calves. The wild red hair and unkempt beard did little to hide the protruding forehead and steely jaw, and the long arms covered in downy red hair lent the illusion of a great ape mimicking human form. Worst of all, he was barefoot, his great feet spread wide in a stance like that of a bare-knuckle boxer, poised to strike; except no boxer would get into a circle with *this* giant.

This was Edward Hyde, but not as I had dreamed in my wildest and most feverish imaginings. He was real.

"Meet Finn, recently from Dungannon," said the boy as he stepped aside. "A genuine Irish giant."

With a stroke of his great arm, Finn took the wind from me as his hand grasped me, sweeping me from my feet and up into the air. It was like being a porcelain doll lifted from a child's bed. The grip, joined by that of his second hand, tightened around me as he swung me over his shoulder and turned to leave the courtyard. My vision blurred as I could make out the boy and Maggie McMahon looking on. While she wore a look of concern upon her face, the brother—for I had concluded he must be such—simply smiled as the courtyard disappeared behind me.

It was a short journey, and one that ended with me raised high over the edge of a bridge, held dangling like a baby from the immense grasp of this monstrous giant. For a moment I was suspended there, looking down upon him, my eyes drawn to the great feet that stood, exposed, upon the cobbles. Then I looked up, into his eyes. There was sadness there, not violence; an expression of duty and, perhaps, a hint of remorse. Even this great beast was no Edward Hyde, and in that I took great comfort.

***

The fall was a short one, maybe fifteen feet. It left me struggling in a mix of mud and raw sewarge as I struggled to find enough water to swim ashore. I was cold and I was wet, but I was *invigorated*. My wretched life had been spared, and my worst nightmare had been brought to life, only to be cast aside (as had my own frail body).

As I pulled myself ashore, I realized that nothing is for nothing, and that somehow, this darkest of encounters had given me hope. Even better, the rush of energy caused by the experience meant I was back at the hotel long before I realised I had not needed my stick.

CHEAPSIDE & HIGHGATE

To the west of Digbeth, from the Markets to the outer ring road, lie Cheapside and Highgate. Divided by Bradford Street, which runs parallel with Digbeth High Street, this part of town retains the dense mix of industrial and residential buildings that were lost in the 1950s when the last of the back-to-back houses there were vacated.

Home to much of the city's Irish community, and to the many gang members of the late nineteenth century (*see Appendix II: Law & Order*), Cheapside continues to serve the businesses of Digbeth, but instead of cheap immigrant housing, workhouses and homeless centres, Bradford Street has been targeted by developers to create attractive city apartments intended to appeal to the burgeoning creative community of Digbeth. With thousands of residential planning approvals for new homes, only the Recession and the housing slump of the mid-noughties have slowed its growth, forcing developers to suspend projects or to rent out apartments for innovative uses such as hen parties until the market recovers. Beyond Bradford Street, city plans are afoot to create a tree-lined urban boulevard cutting through the suburbs to link the city centre with Highgate Park on the edge of the ring road.

OXFORD STREET

Returning along Digbeth High Street, we pass Oxford Street which ends with the *Old Wharf Inn*, one of the younger corner pubs (only dating back to the1920s) which lies at the very heart of old Digbeth. As the town expanded, its industry was pushed back from the causeway and into the side streets. By the nineteenth century the many tanneries, mills and forges had given way to Birmingham's back-to-backs, which combined housing and workshops, ringed around communal courtyards. While most of these were demolished in the 1950s to make way for more commonplace industrial units, a few back-to-backs remain in Birmingham, managed by the National Trust, but there are none left in Digbeth.

HEAVY METAL

This story was originally going to be called On Yer Bike, which was the catch-phrase of Midlands DJ Tony Butler, but in the end we needed somewhere to point out that metal legend Ozzy Osbourne briefly worked in Digbeth, and that Black Sabbath guitarist Tony Iommi's grandfather ran an ice cream shop in Banbury Street when it was part of the Italian Quarter. It's also very slightly steampunk.

"Well, Walter," said I, standing back to admire the fruits of my labours. The delicately interlocking gears gleamed under the flickering light of the workshop bullseye. "What do you think?"

"It's not exactly Brumagem." Walter said as he adjusted his goggles. He peered closely at the intricate detailing of my handiwork as his hands traced the leather upholstery of the spring-mounted seat, ran along the processed aluminium frame that held it all together, and rested, gently, upon the sweeping curve of the steering bar. "It looks... well, artistic"

"That's because it *is* art. Seven years' worth of work went into that."

"But it's just a glorified dandy-horse!"

"Velocipede, Walter." I corrected. "It's a velocipede."

"Looks more like a centipede," he retorted. "I mean, how many wheels does a man need?"

"They're not wheels," I corrected him. "Not all of them. They're cogs! Synchronized gears, in fact. A delicate network designed to amplify the speed.

"Delicate is hardly the word I'd use for something you'd ride over the cobbles of Brum, I can tell you; and those spokes—they're too thin. The slightest knock and they'll be out of shape. Then what will you do?"

It was a fair point. Fosdyke's Dynamic Velocerator might well be the fastest self-propelled vehicle ever invented, but the testing required a long flat track with a very large pile of cushioned boxes at the end. With more than a dozen wheels I'd not yet worked out how the braking mechanism might function, but the device was little more than a means to an end.

"One demonstration will be all I need, Walter," I boasted. "My crowning achievement is, after all, chemical rather than mechanical."

"There must be some better way of demonstrating a.lubricant."

"*Frictionless* lubricant, Walter. Thus reducing wear and tear whilst allowing even the slightest pressure to accelerate the velocerator to unimaginable speeds. On a flat track it will outpace a locomotive, I'm certain of it. That's why the I've booked the Curzon goods yard first thing Monday—it's the perfect place to demonstrate it."

"Look," said Walter, "I'm a manufacturer, and I want to protect my investment. The lubricant is yours, but you promised me the machine. If it can't withstand more than a single journey then I don't see how—"

"Enough, Walter!" I raised my hand. "We made a bargain, and I intend to honour it. Now that the prototype is complete, I have myself an appointment with a forge-master."

"Ah," said Walter, pausing for my explanation. "A local forge-master?"

"Indeed," I agreed. "He has a foundry down by the Grand Union. One of the old rolling mills. He's agreed to smelt a revolutionary new alloy, just for me."

"That's what you said when you made me buy all that aluminium! And see how the price has dropped since I invested—"

"I know, I know, but this is different... it's a local secret."

"How secret?"

"I met a man in a pub..."

"Gah! Men in pubs are no good..."

"A Digbeth Pub. The *Forge*, in fact."

"Oh? And this man you met?"

"A smith," I confirmed. "Calls himself Mr. Wayland. He's asked that I deliver the velocipede this very night."

"In Digbeth? On a Friday night?"

His expression said *are you mad?* I could hardly argue. With drunks on the street, piss-poor lighting and more shadows than a forest at midnight, even the police wouldn't venture out alone, especially without a well-oiled bullseye and a truncheon poised to brain at the first sign of trouble.

"I'll be alright," I said, as much for my benefit as that of Walter. "I'll be heading out at close to midnight, and I've already paid for a slogger escort."

"Sloggers?" He eyed me warily. "They'll mug you as much as look at you."

"It was good money. Five pounds in advance, with the rest payable upon my safe return."

Walter harrumphed at that, but he knew as well as I that there was honour among thieves. Warped honour, perhaps, but a paid-for-job was as good as a banker's draft. He helped me guide my contraption from the workshop. We draped it in the makeshift cover I had fashioned before I set off, on foot. I was tempted to ride the thing, but its fragility was at the forefront of my thoughts. Passing down the Soho Road by the light of the moon, it took three quarters of an hour before I reached the top of the High Street. Looking down into the valley, I could see that last orders had long-since been called, and a couple of weary drinkers meandered across the road towards their Cheapside back-to-backs, one of whom could be heard belting out the chorus of *Champagne Charlie*.

Another two minutes went by and I arrived at my destination, on the corner of Oxford Street, where the sloggers were due to meet me. Sure enough, my escort was waiting on me at the junction. Two boys who, from the flat caps and knotted daffs, I took to be apprentice sloggers. They couldn't have been older than eleven, and their shorts and lack of bother boots marked them as raw recruits rather than the hardened bully boys I had expected.

"Are you here to take me to Mister Wayland?" I asked.

"'tay we," the boys chorused, holding tightly onto their caps and pouting. They hadn't quite mastered the art of looking innocent, and in these streets, such a thing would be a bloody miracle.

By the accent they were probably Staffies from the west, but you could never be sure. With all the Irish and the Italians in the area, the only currency outside of their own was the accent. The low Brumagem dialect came, so I was told, from speaking under the sounds of the forge. There was no point trying to compete by the clang of a hammer or the staccato of a steam engine, so the lower register made more sense. At night, when most of the factory noises died down, you could always tell the newcomers apart, because they hadn't learned the art of the gentle mumble. For a town with so many people, the bustle was quieter and less annoying than in Liverpool or London.

"Darn theer," one of them pointed, indicating the next street corner along where, in the shadows of a railway arch, I could just make out the shadow of another slogger.

With a polite salute I left the boys and pushed the velocipede along the pavement, avoiding the treacherous cobbles. I was fortunate that the click of the spokes and the hiss of the pistons that connected the wheel-pairs together didn't carry so well once I'd entered the street. Rammed full with five to a room in most places, the back-to-backs of Digbeth soaked up the noise as I approached my shadowy liaison.

"Are you for Mister Wayland?" I asked.

"Hssst." Said the boy. "You don't wanna go mentionin' 'is name too freely."

Stepping out into the light, my slogger escort was older—at least fifteen—and, by the cut of his trousers and the weight of his boots, well established within the gang. Escorting me along the street, he tipped his hat as we passed a corner inn. There were still patrons hanging around the doorway, and they all went quiet as we passed them by. Respect on the street would keep me free of trouble, I was sure.

After a few hundred yards we were in the heart of the area, with singers and drinkers all around us. Guiding me behind a stationary dray, the slogger paused beneath one of the Railway viaducts, which was thick with shadows. Knocking on the wooden door of an arch yard, there was a brief exchange and the boy touched his cap before skipping off into the darkness.

The door stood ajar, and inside I saw another shadowy figure, which I took to be another slogger.

"I'm here for Mister Wayland," I whispered, mindful that the name should not be spoken aloud.

The gruff Irish voice that answered me was not that of a boy at all, but of a full grown man... well, a fully adult man. Stepping from the shadows, he was all of three feet tall and dressed like a gypsy. His shaggy white mane and a beard that grew down to his belly gave him the appearance of a Wagnerian dwarf, but his pipe and pork pie hat were of an altogether more recent time.

"The name's Dubh," he said. "Foller me..."

Passing under the Railway viaduct, Dubh led me into a blacksmith's yard, guiding me past kilns and crucibles, anvils and stacks of metal ingots until we came, at last, to a wide well used— no doubt—for quenching the metal. Beside it lay a large, grey, muzzled dog. A Wolfhound I presumed. It rose as we approached, standing a full head taller than Dubh, who scratched beneath its chin in a familiar manner which curbed the growl that has been rising in its throat. As the dog stepped aside, Dubh reached for the lip of the well, grasping one of its uppermost bricks and pulling it aside. As he did so, a grating noise followed and the front of the well slid open. As the bricks ground apart a dark slope emerged; the ringing sound of a tap-hammer echoed through the yard like the staccato beat of a military drum.

Pushing my velocipede onto the incline, we slid beneath the black brick of the viaduct wall and descended into Mister Wayland's forge. Here I saw shallow pools of water interspersed with cauldrons of running metal, white hot from the sweltering furnaces that lined the chamber.

Dubh scuttled ahead of me, passing row upon row of dwarfish smiths, each working an anvil of his own in an industrious crescent of tool-stacked benches and freshly worked metals. As he led me past, I looked to their anvils, and I could see that they were hammering out things familiar to me. Tubes and gears, wheel-rims and screws. Following Dubh, somewhat incredulously, I almost crashed into the back of my host. Mister Wayland.

He was tall—exceptionally tall—well over seven feet high, which made him seem like a giant compared to his diminutive workforce.

"I am Wayland," he said, with a gruffer voice than Dubh, spoken from beneath a longer, darker beard. "You are the inventor?"

I nodded, speechless as he placed his mighty hammer to one side and plunged his thickly calloused hands into a bowl of cooling water. Steam rose as he did so, before withdrawing them and pulling out a white towel with which he wiped the soot and sweat from his hands.

"B-Basil Upton Fosdyke, sir," I stuttered, forcing back my nerves.

He eyed me like a jeweller would appraise a rough-cut lump of rock, and then he eyed my velocipede. I pulled back the tarpaulin to reveal the gradiated rows of wheels and gears which in turn reflected the light of the forge fires. Reaching into his leather apron, Mister Wayland withdrew a thick blueprint—a copy of the design that I had drafted all those years ago. Opening it out, he reoriented it and glanced between the plan and the finished article.

"A good job," he said at last. "Leave it with me, and by tomorrow you shall have a newer, stronger model that will withstand the rigours of the road."

As he turning away from me, I realised that my audience was already over, and Dubh was waiting to escort me from the forge.

***

As an engineer, I spent much of the next day trying to come to terms with what I had seen in Wayland's cave. I'd dropped the "Mister" along with my agnosticism. I was in no doubt that I had not encountered a man, but a demi-god, the sacred smith of old England, and the maker of gifts for the gifted. They say Brunel once struck a deal with Wayland, and Maudslay before him, and Harrison before him. Here, at the heart of industrial Birmingham, was the Empire's greatest secret. The god of engineers.

That evening, as the moon rose high over the city, I departed the workshops that filled Walter's manufactory yard, and made my way back down the Soho Road and into the city once more. Again I met with the sloggers, and again I was led to Dubh, who led me into the concealed yard once more and down beneath the well. As we entered the forge I saw that Wayland was awaiting my arrival, his hand gently resting on the steering bar of a newer, stronger, velocipede.

"It is cooled now, and ready for you to take away," he said as a matter of fact. "I admire your work, Mr Fosdyke, and I hope good things will come to you. But I have one question before you leave."

"Oh, certainly," I said, being as jovial as I dared. "Unless you want me to divulge a trade secret."

Wayland smiled. "I just want to know why there is no braking mechanism fitted. It seems to me that this device might revolutionise transport for centuries to come, but with no brake—"

"I need it for just one demonstration," I replied. "With it, Fosdyke's Frictionless Lubricant will achieve greater success than any simple pedal cycle."

"Ah, yes," said Wayland. "About that—you have my payment?"

I drew from my pocket a vial of the prized lubricant.

"You're sure this is just for personal use?" I asked, handing it over to the great smith, who simply nodded his agreement before releasing the new velocipede into my possession.

"You'll find it is a sturdy metal," he explained. "Harder than any you will have encountered before, for it is the heaviest metal known to all the gods."

Taking up the steering bars, I felt the heft of the new cycle, staggering under the weight as I started to push it up the slope. Each step was leaden, and my muscles strained as I forced it up the gradient, pausing to rest as Dubh and I returned to the yard.

"I hadn't expected—" I began.

"You wanted the sturdiest metal," said Dubh. "You should have expected it to be heavy too."

"It's like lead," I replied. "I'll never push it all the way home."

"That metal," said Dubh, curtailing any dissent, "is forged from the sun of *Svartalfheim* itself. It cannot be broken. It will withstand any impact, weather any blow."

He bowed low as he closed the arched door behind me, and I was left alone on the cobbles with my velocipede. I sighed. It seemed I would have to test Fosdyke's Frictionless Lubricant a little early if I was to get back to my workshop in good time. Hoisting myself up onto the saddle seat, I drew out a vial of the lubricant from my coat, and filled the small concave reservoir set into the steering column.

Pushing the velocipede forwards, I clattered across the cobbles, straining to push down on the heavy pedals. As they completed their first rotation, I felt the gears give and the lubricant glide into place; then I was away, slipping forwards towards the High Street and accelerating as I went.

Skidding into a tight right turn—something I'd not considered for what was, in effect, a straight line cycle—I found that my second push against the pedal kick-started a forward motion that belied the heaviness of the metal. Gathering momentum I ploughed upwards along the High Street, past the markets and out into Dale End. I was cruising away from Digbeth with the hiss of pistons straining to keep up with the rotation of the wheels and gears. The click-click sound of interlocking teeth was gone as the thin, viscous fluid I had introduced made the cycle eat the road. I struggled with a left turn and a later dogleg until I was cruising back up the Soho Road towards the manufactory.

"Wheeeee—" the excitement was overwhelming as I attempted to judge my speed. I was at least matching that of a horse at full canter, and only the vibration of the broad wheel rims provided any discomfort, but not so much as getting saddle-sore from a long horse ride.

Passing Soho House I turned slightly to the left again, cresting the brow of—*the hill*. I cursed. Travelling uphill had been at least manageable, but the velocipede had never been designed to travel downhill. As I fell forwards with the vehicle's momentum our speed surged, and I knew I would be lucky to live long enough to make the test. It was turning into a black Sabbath.

Wrestling with the steering bar to keep it straight, I considered my options as the foundries, the houses and the fields sped past me. Four horses could not have caught me now, plummeting, almost uncontrollably, towards the dip ahead.

With a whoosh, the velocipede and I passed through a shallow puddle as the angle of descent turned into one of ascent, plunging upwards towards the Chamberlain estates. It occurred to me then that I was destined to fly, and a moment later my velocipede was launched upwards in a graceful arc that lifted me high into the air. Up, over terraces and the canal that lay beyond, then down towards certain death. I skimmed trees as the velocipede's speed offered me a hint of salvation: the Reservoir!

Falling free of my invention, I dropped backwards and down, plunging into the icy waters as Wayland's gift smacked into the hard water plane, bisecting it and boring deep beneath the surface. Exhilarated, numbed and in shock, I pulled myself from the great pool that had saved my life. I had overshot the manufactory, and was as far from home as when I had left the the forge. Staggering ashore, I checked my pockets. The lubricant was still there, the glass unbroken, the seal intact. As I sat upon the shore I considered my experience. Science and religion, I realised, just don't mix well.

Taking out the vial, I unstoppered it, and poured the liquid into the still waters of the reservoir. The world wasn't ready for that invention.

Not until I'd built a better bicycle.

MILK STREET

Peter Ackroyd's *The English Ghost* recounts the story of a mysterious and terrible scream often heard in the early hours by constables on the beat in Digbeth. According to this account the scream has been heard in the 1850s, at the turn of the century, and in the 1920s.

Said to come from the vicinity of Milk Street, the scream is attributed to the Battle of Kempe's Hill where the Moore family, who lived in a Milk Street cottage, refused to leave their home when Prince Rupert's army marched upon the Bordesley Bridge. As the Battle of Birmingham raged, it is said that Rupert's men committed a number of atrocities, and that one of these occurred when Moore, his wife and five children were said to have been dragged out of the cottage, one by one and beheaded.

The last of the victims, Moore's thirteen year old daughter, is said to have screamed uncontrollably while her kin were slaughtered, and that her cries were silenced when her own head was severed from her neck.

Another possible solution to the mystery lies with the activities of Birmingham's street gangs, one of which was the Milk Street Gang (*see Appendix II: Law & Order*). Just as the police used whistles to call for assistance, it was common for gang culture to use hoots, howls, screams or other strange noises to warn others that the police were coming. As the gang was active for most of the nineteenth and into the early twentieth century, his relatively mundane explanation cannot be so easily discounted.

THE INSTITUTE & THE BULL'S HEADS

The history of Digbeth is often filled with irony, and the story of the *Digbeth Institute* is no exception, as what was once a building intended to promote temperance and morality became a licensed premises that helped spawn the modern rave and other electronic music scenes.

In the late nineteenth century the temperance movement was particularly active in Digbeth, which had a reputation for unruly behaviour linked to poverty and hard drinking. The Digbeth Institute, designed by Arthur Harrison, opened in January 1908 and was set between two popular local drinking establishments – the *Old Bull's Head* (also known as the *Little Bull's Head*) and the Big Bull's Head.

The Digbeth Institute (right) alongside the Kerryman (middle) and the Big Bull's Head (left).

At the time Digbeth High Street was awash with pubs (In 1861, for example, there was an entire row of pubs lining the High Street: the *King's Head*, the *Horse & Jockey*, the *White Lion*, the *Horse & Groom*, the *Bull's Head*, the *New Bull's Head*, the *Unicorn*, the *Three Tuns* and the *Talbot*). As the names suggest these pubs were associated with horse racing and, in particular, with its associated gangs (*see Appendix II: Law & Order*).

Now known as the *Kerryman*, the *Bull's Head* was built in the middle of the eighteenth century becoming the *Old Bull's Head* when the *Big Bull's Head* appeared in the nineteenth century. Both lively Irish locals, the pubs have continued to thrive through their proximity to the *Institute* and the Coach Station opposite, for which they were treated as unofficial waiting rooms.

Sponsored by Carr's Lane Church, the *Digbeth Institute* provided classes for poor children, as well as offering space for society meetings—particularly for the local temperance society—in an attempt to provide an alcohol free environment for the women of a parish well known for its drunks. These activities continued until 1954 when, with the area's declining population and the shift to industrial use, it was sold to Birmingham City Council, who used is as Digbeth's Civic Hall for a number of years. As a venue used for various concerts, the Institute appealed to music promoters, and evolved into the original *Godskitchen* super club. Its presence attracted a thriving rave community to the area, which has continued even after the club vacated the site and it passed into the hands of new developers. From 2010, the *Institute* has been a major 2,900 capacity music venue, making it a major contributor to the UK concert circuit.

FLOODGATE STREET

The creation of a gravel causeway to raise the street level in medieval times helped contain the River Rea's flood waters, but led the rural meadows that lay along old Water Street to become waterlogged, forming pools that attracted mills, tanyards and iron foundries to the area. This watercourse, possibly known as the dyke's path or the duck's bath, is cited as the origin of the name Digbeth.

The River Rea at Floodgate Street.

Up until the sixteenth century the river split into two watercourses—the Rea (spanned by a stone bridge) and the Deritend Brook, spanned by a ford—forming a small island. By the seventeenth century the ford was also covered and the Deritend island obscured. The road that passed over it was divided between the boggy Digbeth causeway (heading towards the town proper) and a drier mud Holloway that passed through Deritend and up towards Camp Hill.

Heavy use of the Rea for industry and the disposal of human waste led to the introduction of floodgates c.1649, but these did little to prevent a series of heavy floods throughout the nineteenth century, which turned much of the already inadequate housing of the area into little more than an open sewer. Culverts were added to better control the water-flow, and Water Street subsequently became known as Floodgate Street.

BORDESLEY BRIDGE

Looking uphill, towards Bordesley and Camp Hill, we are surrounded by what remains of the conflict between the workers of Birmingham and the Royalist army of Prince Rupert of the Rhine. This incident was of great significance to the outcome of the English Civil War, using Prince Rupert's treatment of Birmingham's defenders as a propaganda victory that bolstered support for the Parliamentarian cause.

Many of the area's ghost stories hark back to the events of April 1643, a fuller account of which is given at *Appendix I: The Battle of Kempe's Hill*. One tragic event recalls how, in 1789, a Mr Wright, while attempting to cross the Bordesley Bridge fell into the Rea where he died, smothered by the mud.

THE BATTLE OF BORDESLEY BRIDGE

Traditional ghost stories involve places haunted by ghosts in stories like the Milk Street Scream. However, as Lynn M. Cochrane shows us, it is equally possible for the ghosts themselves to be haunted by the places...

It was Richie who inspired us—Captain Richard Greaves, that is. Not far short of "sir" as far as I'm concerned, although we're not supposed to use foul language like that any more.

I remember him calling us together, just after he'd marched in with the two hundred troops of the Lichfield garrison, coming from King's Norton. He reckoned the Royalists were on their way towards us. Well, we weren't having any of their fancy nonsense! Not a hope. Parliament had a much better idea of how we should be governed. None of us were prepared to make swords or halberds or muskets or cannon or shot for the Papist-leaning king of England, Scotland and Wales. Nor any of his pompous henchmen!

Why should we? We were all free, craftsmen and tradesmen, good, honest, free, English, working families. And it was the families; men, women and children, each doing their bit. Chain making. Nail making. Hammering out the iron-work for farms and armies alike. Most of us had a timber-framed house at the front and a little brick-built forge at the back and the ringing of hammers on anvils marked out the hours of daylight and sometimes haunted the air long into the night.

Air? Huh! The stuff we breathed day by day could hardly be called air! Our homes were, at best, two-tone black. Smoke curled and wafted through and round the streets - and that was on a good day. On a day when rain tried to wash the air clean, everything got covered in a layer of grime. It was the Dirty End of town, Deritend, just across the Bordesley Bridge, over the River Rea from Digbeth.

Richie wandered up and down the High Street; Digbeth, over Bordesley Bridge, Deritend, as far as Kempe's Hill and the *Old Ship Inn*. He must have been looking for a sensible place to build defences because he suddenly got us digging, even though it was late on Easter Sunday, throwing up an earthen bank across the causeway just on the Digbeth side of Bordesley Bridge.

I helped, of course, and again on the Monday morning before I got sent up to lie near the eaves of my home, in between Gibb Street and the river, with my musket ready to fire.

"We'll hold them up at the bridge," Richie said. "It doesn't matter how many of them there are, there are three hundred of us and they can only cross the bridge one or two at a time. When the two hundred regulars have got them penned by the bridge, you locals fire at them. You'll be hidden in your homes. Perfectly safe. We can stop them here. Bordesley Bridge will be famous because of the bravery of the men, and women, of Deritend, Digbeth and Birmingham."

We believed him, of course, and went up into our roof-spaces with our muskets, powder and shot. There were even one or two armed with antique bows and arrows. We were on Prince Rupert's side of the river. We had to be if we were to kill Royalists waiting to cross over the bridge.

And then the Royalists decided that we were going to look after them!

A small band of them arrived, knocking on every door as they made their way down the street, informing us that soldiers were to be billeted in our homes. I heard them coming down Holloway, hammering on doors, including mine. Verity, my wife, had the door already barricaded shut, of course. It creaked a bit but it held.

"Give us quarters," came the cry from outside. "Look after our worthy gentlemen and no harm will be done to you. You have nothing to fear from our soldiers. Open your doors to us."

From what I heard, perched silently above the street, my neighbours were quite inventive about denying them as much as a drop of water or a crumb of bread, let alone quarters. I would have denied them life itself! Verity gave as good as anyone else. I was so proud of her, barely sixteen and already swelling with our first child.

I heard the feet march away, back towards the *Old Ship Inn*, and called Verity to the foot of the ladder I had used to reach my vantage point.

"Verity, my sweetest," I said, "go now, quickly, while there are no Royalists around. Go to your parents' and get them and your sisters to leave. It isn't safe, whatever people might say. Go and look after our baby and I'll join you as soon as I can."

"You're sending me back to my parents'?" asked Verity. "I'm married to you. I stay with you!"

"I'm asking you to do a job I can't do, to be the other side of the coin for me. Get your parents and sisters to safety," I said. "I'm staying here to get rid of any Royalists that dare to stop where I can get a clear shot at them."

She blew me a kiss but the look on her face said she was being tortured.

"I love you, sweetness," I said. "Be me where I can't be."

She clattered out of sight, went out through the forge door and slithered between our house and our neighbour's. I heard her voice ring clear to those guarding the bridge a few moments later.

"It's Verity Chinn, Verity Moore, as was. I'm going to Milk Street to get my parents and sisters," she yelled. "You've known me long enough, Simon Miller. Let me pass!"

I grinned at her words. Simon had grown up with us, playing games in the streets. Now that game was war. Verity's footsteps crossed the bridge and soon I heard her father greet her. Then it went quiet.

I resumed my watch of the street, ready and waiting. After all, what chance did the fancy Royalists have against brave, free men?

What chance did brave, free men have against sneaky, despicable Royalists who changed the rules of war to suit themselves?

I heard him myself! The fancy boy was on horseback, a sturdy mount from what I could see, and he sat on his horse, by the bridge, urging his men to cross. He was just out of range of my musket!

Our side shot volley after volley, stopping the much bigger force at the bridge and those of us in the houses tried to pick off individuals that could go no further.

They fell back, regrouped, while our lads reloaded and got ready again.

They charged for a second time but, oddly, there didn't seem so many of them.

Once more they fell back.

But then I saw what the sneaky rebels had done. Across the fields, on the far side of the river, horsemen came galloping at the unprotected backs of Richie's men. They had no choice. They fell back through Digbeth and up into Birmingham town itself.

And we were left stranded.

We were also under orders. We shot at anything that stood still long enough for us to have a clear target.

Perhaps we should have fled with our wives and children. Some did. Perhaps they were the wise ones. I didn't, lining up shot after shot as horsemen and dragoons and foot-soldiers went past.

Eventually, I heard, in an exasperated tone, "Fire the houses they're shooting from!"

Even then I could have left!

But I chose to stay, giving Verity as much time as possible to escape, taking out as many as I could of the fancy Royalists.

The acrid smell of burning thatch alerted me. The roof had caught fire in several places. I ran for my life - and tripped to fall headlong down the ladder from the roof space.

And Verity's scream filled my ears.

When I came to, I had double vision and a thumping headache - a headache that rang to the sound of a forge. With one eye, I could see the forge, and a man pounding away on the lump of iron on his anvil, not me but doing my job. With the other eye, I could still see the street outside, busy by day and night with horses and carts going up and down the Holloway or turning into Gibb Street.

The fact that I wasn't breathing any more didn't worry me. The air had always been thick enough to eat.

Nor was I worried when fashions changed and the people paraded around in outrageous clothing.

And from time to time, from across the river, rang the sound of Verity's scream.

The forge fell silent after a while but the earth-shaking pounding didn't stop. It grew deeper, louder, made of sterner stuff. I began to feel pressure, pushing me down into the mud that has always lined the banks of the River Rea.

I lost sight of my forge, partly, perhaps, because I was no longer looking in the same direction. The bridge was a little nearer—as if I was now somewhere under where my neighbour's house had stood, although there seemed to be no building on me and the pounding came from one side. I wriggled a little, got my musket into position to fire. I was still under orders, after all. I just hadn't seen any Royalists recently.

Slowly, I realised that even the horses were becoming fewer. No one was riding over the bridge—Bordesley Bridge, the bridge we'd tried so hard to defend. Perhaps we'd won. Perhaps it hadn't all been in vain. I never did find out. Perhaps it didn't matter...

I blanked that thought at once. If Royalists didn't ride horses any more, what did they ride?

Perhaps it was the large carriages that took a whole army of people at a time.

I changed my mind soon after. Royalists always wore fancy clothes, specially made, only-one-of-this-type garments. The people festooned on and in these carriages were almost in uniform, drab, grey-brown, all much the same.

Perhaps it was the tall wheels with the little trailing wheel.

I changed my mind again. Far too many of the riders fell off into the mud - and it wasn't what you might call clean mud! I'd emptied enough night-soil into the roadway in my time! Royalists wouldn't have lowered themselves to decorating their fancy raiment with the stinking result that formed the main part of the carriageway.

Perhaps it was the huffing and puffing contraptions that moved without horses.

Again, I changed my mind. The monstrous machines were far too unwieldy, clanking along, puffing out smoke that seemed worse than the worst my little forge had ever spewed out. These horseless vehicles were surely never for the likes of the Royalists, dirty and smutty as they were. Although, with my other eye, I watched building behind me, arch after arch, until a clanking, thundering version, spitting sparks and belching fumes, rushed past, overhead.

Perhaps the long string of carriages it pulled would be a place Royalists would travel.

Again, I watched carefully, looking for evidence.

And again I changed my mind. The carriages were usually full but the army that filled them ranged from tiny babies to people too old, surely, to still be alive. No Royalists, there. These carriages were full of ordinary people, people much like me and mine. Free men and women, crafts and trades, earning an honest penny or two to sustain life.

I waited. I'd find those Royalists yet—those Royalists that had made my Verity's scream echo through time!

Fashions changed again. Women exposed so much flesh, at times, I wondered if they were walking around in their undergarments. Men, too, flaunted sleek bodies, skin tanned beyond belief but nothing to suggest real hard work. Were these the Royalists? Maybe not. Royalists had to flaunt not just themselves but how enabled they were to acquire anything they wanted. Bluntly, Royalists exuded cash.

I watched. From time to time, Verity's scream sundered the air, shook me to the depths of my soul. Patience, Verity, my sweetness, I will join you as soon as I run out of shot.

The vehicles changed. Heavy, road-shaking goods vehicles, streams of smaller horseless carts and communal carriages by day and for the earlier part of the night. Fewer vehicles, of a different type in the later part of the night.

And then I realised. The new Royalists are chasing each other out along the causeway and up the Holloway in the small, noisy horseless carts that light the roadway below them in shades of blue, green and red. Sometimes, they wait for each other right in front of me, between Bordesley Bridge and Gibb Street.

And I have one last shot in my musket.

THE FLOODGATE STREET SCHOOL

Recently renovated, extended and reopened as the main Digbeth campus of *South Birmingham College* (now *South & City College*), the Floodgate Street Boarding School, well known for its artistic towers, gables, red brick and terracotta style, was originally built in 1891. Commissioned by the Birmingham School Board to accommodate the poor children of Digbeth it was, despite its size, intended to educate over a thousand pupils. During the second world war it suffered bomb damage and was taken over by St. Michael's Roman Catholic Church which in turn became, in 1982, an annexe of *Hall Green Technical College*.

The Floodgate Street School.

THE JFK MEMORIAL

Commissioned and funded by the Irish community, the John F Kennedy Memorial Mosaic, rededicated in February 2013, now stands on the corner of Floodgate Street beside the old works entrance to Devonshire Works, and opposite the Irish Centre and Connaught Square.

Originally erected outside St. Chad's Roman Catholic Cathedral in July 1968, the mosaic celebrated the lives of Kennedy, the American Irish, and other champions of freedom such as the Rev.

Martin Luther King. The original mosaic bore the legend "There are no white or coloured signs on the graveyards of battle".

Removed for street improvements in 2007, it re-emerged in Digbeth with a new face on the mosaic—that of the city's first Irish Lord Mayor, Mike Angle.

The John F. Kennedy Memorial Mosaic, relocated to Digbeth in 2013.

From Floodgate Street we return to the Custard Factory and the Old Crown, with plenty of places to rest weary feet, find food, drink, and even a room for the night.

WEIRD TRAILS 1

APPENDICES

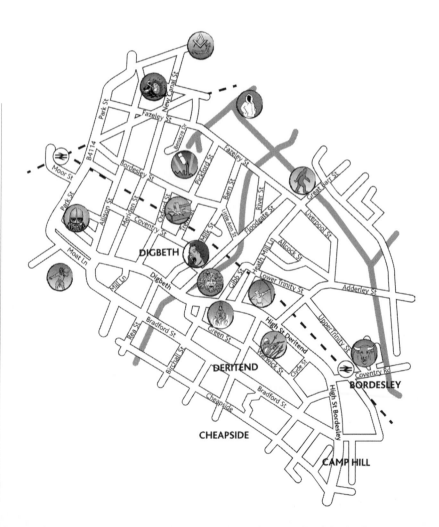

I. THE BATTLE OF KEMPE'S HILL

When Rupert came to Birmingham,
We were in sorry plight.
Our blood God's earth did stain every day,
Our homes in blazing ruins lay,
And stained the sky at night.
With matchlock and with culverin,
With caliver and drake,
He shot our sons and fathers down,
And hell on earth did make.
Our children's cries, our widows' prayers,
Ascended with the flame,
And called down the wrath divine
Upon the Royal murderer's line,
And brought his kin to shame

—*The Armourer's Widow*

Image of Rupert in Birmingham, from a Commonwealth pamphlet, The Cruel Practices of Prince Rupert, 1643.

Prior to the battle, Prince Rupert's army, which numbers some 1,200 cavalry and dragoons and 6-700 foot had three objectives: clear the countryside as much as possible, punish Birmingham, and then take the garrison at Lichfield in readiness for the King's arrival. To this end they rapidly passed through the Midlands, travelling from Oxford to Birmingham in just three days. On the afternoon of the 3rd April 1643 his army reached the junction of the Stratford and Warwick Roads, whereupon he despatched his quartermaster to the edge of Birmingham. Here, at a place known as Kempe's Hill, an offer was made to the people of Birmingham. They were told that if they conducted themselves peaceably and provided lodgings for Rupert's army, then they would not be made to suffer for their past mistakes.

These 'past mistakes' involved the forging of swords and supplying them to Cromwell's army. Understandably, the workers of Birmingham found such an offer hard to believe, and decided to refuse to give the king any quarter inside the town.

At this point, according to a pamphlet called *The Burning Love*, a man called Whitehale (*"who hath bin long lunatick, held Jewish opinions, and had layn in Bedlam and other prisons (some say) 16, some 22 yeares, and was lately come out."*) spoke out against the King, pouring scorn upon any offer of quarter made by any *"Popish armies or souldiers"*. Believing him to be Francis Roberts, the puritan minister resident at St. Martin in the Bull Ring, the quartermaster's men beat and hacked him to death before threatening repercussions for the town. These threats were met with musket fire.

King Charles' ire over Birmingham's disloyalty was well known, and in expectation of some punishment for their deeds, 300 men had initially been sent from Coventry to reinforce the town. With no sign of the King's armies, these men had returned from whence they came, escorting many who fled Birmingham for fear that a town with only earthworks for defences was sure to fall quickly.

Those who remained did not expect that they would be putting up a fight, intending instead to stand up to the Prince, opposing him with their words rather than by bearing arms. This changed when a force of 200 men, commanded by a Captain Greaves of the Lichfield garrison, who arrived via the nearby town of King's Norton. While most of the workers on the road between Kempe's Hill and the town of Birmingham itself fled with their families into the high town, Greaves and his men, bolstered by around a hundred volunteers armed with makeshift weapons, set up barricades and prepared to defend themselves against the overwhelming might of Prince Rupert's army.

Arriving at the earthworks on which Kempe's Hill was raised, Rupert made his headquarters at the *Ship Inn*, instructing his troops to set up camp on the surrounding hilltop. It is from this point in Birmingham's history that Kempe's Hill came to be known as Camp Hill.

Further downhill, on the muddy Holloway that passed between Bordesley and Deritend, Captain Greaves' Roundheads set up their defences. Bordesley Bridge, which crossed the River Rea, was seen as a natural bottleneck where a few might be able to stand against the many. Setting up a battle line made up of only a few musketeers, the defenders dug in, and waited.

Impatient to punish the town, Prince Rupert gave the order to attack, marching his men into a wall of shot so heavy that, despite their overwhelming numbers, they were forced to retreat. Surprised and a little unnerved, Rupert refused to believe he might not take the town, ordering a second attempt upon the bridge.

Again his forces were repulsed.

The possibility of defeat by what he believed to be simple townsfolk was not something Rupert dared contemplate. With few defences in the surrounding fields, Rupert decided to supplement a third assault with a flanking attack, ordering his dragoons to cross the surrounding meadows and ford the Rea further north, circumventing Greaves' defences and entering the town at Lower Mill Street.

Unable to withstand an assault on two fronts, the defenders abandoned their positions and fled to the high town. Without regrouping, Rupert's troops pursued them, setting fire to houses and workshops from which they had been fired upon. Those who fled were unable to regroup and were forced to scatter as the town burned.

The Burning Love pamphlet describes what happened next:

"The Cavaliers rode up into the Towne like so many Furyes or Bedlams, the Earle of Denbigh being in the front, singing as he rode, they shot at every doore or window where they could espy any looking out, they hacked, hewed, or pistolled all they met with, without distinction, blaspheming, cursing, and damming most hidiously. Discovering a Troope of Horse, which was under the command of Captaine Greaves at the further end of the Towne facing them. They pursued after them, who after a little flight wheeled about, and most stoutly charged them through, and the Captaine received five small wounds (which are now almost well). In which charge the Earle of Denbigh was knockt off his horse, laid for dead, and his pockets rifled (though his wounds not so mortall as to die presently) the rest of his horse were chased till they came neere their own Colours, which was excellent Service, for meane while most of the Townes foot escaped away.

"After which Captain Greaves retreated, and so advanced to Lichfield."

In the wake of the rout:

"Their Horse rode desparatly round the Town, leaping hedges and ditches (wherein one is reported to breake his neck) to catch the Townesmen; no madmen could ride more furiously. They slew in their frenzy as we are informed, about 14 in all."

The next day as they moved on to Lichfield, Rupert's forces plundered and torched a further eighty houses between Bull Street and Moor Street, in accordance with continental rules of war. This led to a public outcry, as such acts were presented as atrocities in England, and a series of pamphlets were released applauding the bravery of the sturdy sons of Birmingham whilst emphasising the cruelty and barbarism of

Rupert's men who caroused, plundered and sacked the town, pausing only to toast the health of "Prince Rupert's Dog".

In all, around 155 houses were burned in the incident—said to account for a third of the town. The bitterness of the locals was such that a week after Christmas that year the townsfolk took revenge by laying seige to the nearby Aston Hall, which they captured.

An engraving of the Chartist Riots of 1839, from Cornelius Brown's *True Stories of the Reign of Queen Victoria*, 1886.

Birmingham's emergence as a city came in the wake of rapid and uncontrollable population growth caused by the Industrial Revolution. To put this into perspective, Birmingham in the eighteenth century underwent a 900% population increase, becoming Britain's third most populous town after London and Bristol. By comparison, the national population increased by only 14%.

The introduction of Street Commissioners by parliament in the 1780s had helped to curb early disturbances, but with only two officers dealing with a population of 50,000 the town soon earned a reputation as a place that couldn't police itself.

As a focus for much of Birmingham's workforce, Digbeth played host to many, many ale houses. This led to a lot of wild and unruly behaviour, and to the formation of various gangs whose associations, though doubtless connected to the pubs and factories, were primarily connected to the streets. As well as matters of public disorder, the gangs, known as sloggers, were heavily involved in brawling, bull-baiting, cock-fighting and pigeon racing, making most of their money from illegal gambling, particularly on the horses.

By November 1839, in the wake of Chartist Riots at the Bull Ring, the Birmingham police were formed. The new force, made up of some 260 men, saw one officer for every 600 citizens. In spite of this, the town simply didn't have the capacity to deal with the scale of criminal activity. Most of the population were housed in dirty, sewage-ridden slums, with thousands living in cramped tenements with shared washrooms and communal toilets. With no sanitised housing until the 1860s, squalor and disease were endemic, it was only a matter of time until the streets erupted with violent conflict. The English sloggers of Cheapside vied with the mostly Irish street gangs of Digbeth—the Milk Street Gang, the Barn Street Gang, the Allison Street Gang, the Park Street Gang and the Peaky Blinders of Adderley Street—for control of the area.

This situation was made worse by a travelling Irish demagogue, William Murphy, who toured England preaching anti-Catholic rhetoric. Following an 1867 speech in Birmingham, in which he labelled the Pope as 'a rag and bone gatherer', the local Irish workforce rioted, wrecking much of Park Street at the top of Digbeth and forcing the police to disperse the crowds with cutlasses. Dubbed the Murphy Riots, the incident forced the Mayor to bolster the police with 600 special constables, 300 soldiers and 100 cavalry. The number of violent assaults, particularly between the English and Irish gangs, rose significantly. In 1868 the police stocked up on guns, pistols and swords, storing them at the nearby Moor Street gaol. By 1874 the sloggers had the upper hand. More riots followed (notably the Navigation Street 'riot of roughs' which saw two police officers stabbed, one of whom died) and by 1876 Public House Inspectors had been introduced in an effort to break the ties between violence and alcohol. In 1879 Birmingham was recorded as the town where the highest proportion of violent deaths occurred.

Of all of Birmingham's gangs, the most well-remembered were Adderley Street's Peaky Blinders, known as such because of their distinctive style of dress. Their hair was cropped short in the prison style, with a 'donkey' forelock swept down above the eyes. Beneath this they wore wide flat caps at a rakish angle. It was common for a cut-throat razor to be concealed, sewn into the peak of the hat so it could be used as a slashing weapon to blind or main. They were also known for wearing a silk daff or scarf around their necks and sporting wide bell-bottoms held up by thick, heavily buckled belts. These buckles were often razor sharp for a similar purpose as the cap, used as flails when roughing it with other gangs. The blinders' territory started in Adderley Street, running up the Coventry Road to Small Heath and Little Bromwich where they were known to extort and mug passers by. Active some time before before 1870 until around 1902, their behaviour was eventually curbed by the work of a local priest, Arnold Pinchard, who introduced the boys to more gentlemanly pursuits, such as boxing.

By the end of the nineteenth century, the situation had begun to ease. City incorporation in 1889 had brought more power to the local politicians, population growth had slowed, the influence of churches and the local temperance movement were starting to have an impact, and the expansion of Birmingham's boundaries in 1891 had led to a corresponding expansion of the police force. In addition, the rise of football clubs like Aston Villa and Small Heath Alliance (now known as Birmingham City) gave the young men something new to focus their energy on.

Of course, it didn't take long for the area's association with crime to resurface, and in the post-war era unlicensed bookmakers emerged as a major problem, particularly at Ascot and Epsom. Turning to the gangs for protection, one of the biggest, based around the pubs lining Digbeth High Street, were the Brummagem Boys. Led by the charming Billy Kimber, they gained notoriety during a bloody clash at the Epsom Derby of 1921. After being deterred by police at the Derby itself, the Brummagem Boys prepared a roadside ambush of London's Sabini Gang (also known as the Italian Mob), but instead waylaid an allied gang, the Leeds Mob, resulting in one death and twenty eight arrests.

Hostilities between the gangs continued until the dawn of the second world war.

III. THE BIRMINGHAM BIGFOOT

Philip John Smith, Serial Killer.

In recent years, Digbeth acquired its very own serial killer. His name was Philip John Smith, and he had been a childhood neighbour of Fred and Rose West before joining Billy Danter's Funfair as a fairground worker at the age of fourteen. Travelling the UK for almost twenty years, he eventually moved to Athlone in Ireland for a time before settling down in Birmingham.

In 1999 Smith took up residence at the Trinity Centre for the Homeless on Bradford Street, which was on the opposite side of the High Street. He would later find a more permanent home in nearby Sparkbrook, but remained unemployed. He took on work as an odd-job man at the *Rainbow* pub on Adderley Street, as well as using his Volvo to provide an unlicensed taxi service.

At a height of six feet four and weighing around 22 stone, Smith had earned the nickname 'Bigfoot' (allegedly because his big feet left black scuff marks everywhere he walked), along with a reputation as a 'gentle giant'.

He and his crimes, however, were far from gentle.

Over a 96 hour period in November 2000, Smith groomed his victims before taking them away to strangle and bludgeon them to death.

His first confirmed victim was 21-year old Jodie Hyde, a local butane addict whom he met at the *Rainbow*. On 9th November 2000 her drove her home to her flat in Alum Rock where he strangled and killed her. Tying her naked body in a blanket, he dumped her on open land at the *Ackers Trust* in Sparkbrook, setting fire to her remains. Her smouldering body, burned almost beyond recognition, was discovered by police in the early hours.

His next victim, just three days later, was 25 year old Rosemary Corcoran. Again, Smith befriended her at the *Rainbow* before moving on for a drink at the *Kerryman* further down the High Street and then on to *Monte Carlo*'s, a nightclub in Handsworth. From there he forced her into his car and drove her twenty miles to an empty lane close to the *Robin Hood* pub in Rashwood, near Droitwich Spa, Worcestershire.

Here he beat her to death and drove over the body as he headed back to Birmingham where, as she walked through Balsall Heath on her way to work at a local care home, 39 year-old Carol Jordan was hit from behind by his Volvo. Collapsing to the ground with a fractured hip, she could offer no resistance as Smith bundled her into the car and drove her to Bell Barn Lane in Lea Bank, where, after beating her until she was unrecognisable, he abandoned the dead body.

Turning himself in before the body of his second victim had even been identified, Smith faced overwhelming police evidence and was sentenced to life imprisonment in July 2001. The police operation, dubbed 'Operation Green', then focused on another possible victim who had died in October 2000.

Patricia Lynott, a 47-year-old mother of two, had been working as a cleaner and child-minder for the landlady of the *Rainbow* when, on 25th October, concerns by her employer and her co-worker, Philip Smith, were raised. They accompanied the police to her flat in Maxstoke Street, Bordesley Green, where her body was found. It was assumed to be natural causes, with an injury sustained to her head attributed to falling out of bed, but Green's killing spree raised suspicions and her body, which had been returned to Ireland for burial, was re-examined. The results were inconclusive, but within three years Operation Green had given way to Operation Enigma, in which more than six police forces re-examined the unsolved murders of between 14 and 40 possible victims stretching back to the 1980s. These women were believed to have been killed by Smith as he toured the country as a fairground worker.

***

While Smith still serves a life sentence for his crimes, an echo of his killing spree perhaps lives on among the streets of Digbeth. In 2010 a local youth arts project, *UnsolvedWM*, investigated a number of local urban legends as well as fabricating some found footage of their own. Among the legends they came across was talk of a 'Birmingham Bigfoot' seen roaming the streets of Digbeth.   Was this, perhaps, inspired by rumours of Philip Smith's days in Digbeth only ten years before?   Alternately, the rumour could have had its origins in the Cannock Chase Bigfoot craze of the mid-noughties. Sightings of a so-called bigfoot at nearby Cannock Chase, where they have been used to big cat sightings over the years, inspired the Chase's locals to don gorilla and Chewbacca suits to prank the rising number of visiting 'bigfoot hunters' to the area. For the Birmingham bigfoot, mock footage of a creature hiding in the bushes of a local cemetery, and of it jumping from Great Barr Street bridge down onto the Grand Union Canal tow-path, have gone viral, leading towards an uneasy conflation of these two, very different, stories. Perhaps Smith's Jekyll-Hyde nature will inspire the next development of the myth.

The Dubliner in the Irish Quarter.

Much of old Irish Birmingham is long gone, but the Irish Quarter still retains its own sense of identity with the Irish Centre, the *Dubliner* (Once known as the *Barrel Organ*, this cavernous bar was at the heart of Birmingham's metal scene in the 1970s and 80s) and the *Kerryman* opposite being the most visible signs of links with the area.

The Irish presence in Digbeth goes back at least as far as the seventeenth century, although at that time Birmingham was a staunchly protestant town. Waves of Irish immigrants began to arrive in the early eighteenth century, to find work as labourers, particularly on the canals and later the railways and, in the 1840s, to escape the Irish potato famine. Taking the roughest work and the lowest wages, they piled into the inner city slums of Cheapside and Digbeth, parts of which were as much as 55% Irish. While other nationalities—notably Italians after the first world war, and Poles after the second—also made their homes in the area, creating a hub of Catholic activity supported by churches like the short-lived Masshouse, St. Michaels' in Albert Street, St. Nicholas' in Park Street and St. Anne's in nearby Alcester Street.

It is perhaps ironic that while the Irish mostly lived in Digbeth, many of the surviving Irish pubs—like the *Anchor* and the *Spotted Dog*—are in Cheapside, on the opposite side of the High Street. This trend has continued with the renaming of the *Barrel Organ* and the building of the Irish Centre and its *Connaught* bar. Indeed the Connaught Square

Development taking place between the High Street and Bradford Street, was part-funded by the Irish Government as a means of reinforcing Digbeth as the community's spiritual home.

Since 1952 Digbeth has played host to an annual St. Patrick's Day Festival, running from Camp Hill, along the High Street and up to Park Street. It is the event most commonly associated with the area, regularly attracting crowds of more than 80,000, becoming the third largest such festival in the world (smaller only than those of Dublin and New York).

The recently rebuilt Birmingham Coach Station that sits alongside the Dubliner and adjacent to Connaught Square, has embraced its Irish links, incorporating the concept of *míle fáilte*—a hundred thousand welcomes—into its redesign.

ACKNOWLEDGEMENTS

As with most urban legends, the primary source for much of the content contained within this book comes from the streets of Digbeth. Conversations in bars or during walks through the area regularly unearth little gems of hidden history and, just as often, misremembered tales that have a flavour of their own. Most of the information here is drawn from notes made over several years, not always identifying the source or veracity of their origins. That said, every effort has been made to the corroborate any information presented as fact, and it is hoped that the various sources are captured within these acknowledgements.

Much of Birmingham's hidden history has resurfaced courtesy of historic writers such as William Hutton (An History of Birmingham, 1781), Charles Pye (*A Description of Modern Birmingham*, 1818), Walter Showell (*Dictionary of Birmingham*, 1885) and Joshua Toulmin Smith (*Memorials of Old Birmingham*, 1863), but in more recent years some significant contributors to our understanding of Birmingham's history stand out among the many local historians without whose often insightful, always entertaining rummagin' round Brummagem, we would have a lot less understanding of the city. They are Carl Chinn, William Dargue, Mike Hodder, Joe Holyoke and Chris Upton. Joe in particular, along with Richard Trengrouse, have been entertaining visitors to Digbeth with their often impromptu walks for a number of years, and much of what is contained herein follows in their footsteps.

For direct assistance with the production of this book, thanks must go to Kate Middleton and Badger, who spent a solid four hours walking the streets of Digbeth securing the many photographs appearing in this volume; for his graphic design skills and creating the walking map and associated images, big thanks also go to Big Beano, aka Mike Watts; and for formatting against the odds, thanks also to Damon Cavalchini. One shot we couldn't quite capture in time was the Digbeth Institute, and we have instead used an image captured by Tim Hisgett in 2010.

Of course, some parts of this book are works of fantasy, pure and simple. In this regard there are those whose input has helped to make this project a reality, and some well deserved thanks are therefore given to: Chris Amies, Steve Bishop, Paul Cornell, Matthew Griffiths, Steve Jones, Roz Kaveney, Joel Lane, John Meaney, Simon Morden, Rosie Pocklington, Mike Shevdon.

I Bought a Vampire Motorcycle © 1990, Dirk Productions Ltd.

Special thanks must also be given to Toin Adams (*www.steelsculpt. com*) for her inspirational works of art and the input she has given (Beorma images © 2009), Toin Adams.

BIOGRAPHIES

One question you may be asking yourselves is "How much of this is true?". Of the walk itself, the facts and anecdotes have been drawn from existing sources—reputable historians on the one hand, and first, second and third hand eyewitnesses on the other. What we can confirm is that the short stories presented by our authors may well be fictitious—but nothing is for certain.

JAMES BROGDEN is a part-time Australian who studied at Birmingham University in the 80's and now lives with his wife and two daughters in Bromsgrove, Worcestershire, where he teaches English. His first published short story, *The Pigeon Bride*, won a competition in the Midlands edition of *The Big Issue* to find a 'modern midlands fable', and in 2012 his first novel, Birmingham-based *The Narrows*, was published by *Snowbooks*. His urban fantasy fiction has since appeared in various anthologies such as the British Fantasy Society's *Dark Horizons, Anachron Press' Urban Occult,* and the *Alchemy Press Book of Ancient Wonders.* His latest novel, *Tourmaline* has just been released, in which Spaghetti Junction becomes the birthplace of an unspeakable evil. Blogging occurs at jamesbrogden. blogspot.co.uk, and tweeting at *@skippybe.*

MIKE CHINN was born in Smethwick, a town which has long struggled with its identity: first it was in the county of Staffordshire; then it became part of Warley, in Worcestershire; presently Sandwell, West Midlands (whilst the outside world believes it to be a suburb of Birmingham). In 1981 he married and moved to Sparkhill, and currently resides with wife Caroline and their clamouring hoard of guinea pigs in Hall Green. Of his 58 years, 32 have been spent as a resident of Birmingham—so Smethwick's plastic geography notwithstanding, he's some sort of Brummie.

He has published over 40 short stories, from Westerns to Lovecraftian fiction; with all shades of Fantasy, Horror, Science Fiction and Pulp Adventure in between—along with the occasional comic strip. His forthcoming Sherlock Holmes Steampunk mash-up from *Fringeworks* sees the famous detective visiting the Moon.

LYNN M. COCHRANE was born and still lives in the outskirts of Birmingham. She has been writing most of her life and has produced three collections of poems. She has had a few short stories published in convention publications, one in *Raw Edge*, the West Midlands Arts publication, one in *The Alchemy Press Book of Ancient Wonders* and one in *Andromeda's Offspring Vol.1*. She taught Geography in Birmingham for many years, including looking at how the village grew into the city as the example of a settlement changing over time. She is a member of Cannon Hill Writers' Group, leading writing workshops from time to time, and is currently editor of their showcase anthology, *Salvo* and their sampler pamphlets *Grapeshot*.

THERESA DERWIN is of Irish descent, having been born and raised in Birmingham, just a couple miles from old Digbeth. With a PGDip in nineteenth century literature she has a special interest in the history of the city, and her short stories often draw on this. Since her short story collection, *Monsters Anonymous*, was published by *Anarchy Books* in 2012, she has gone a bit barmy, taking on an imprint of her own (*KnightWatch Press*), editing four anthologies (with more to come), and setting up *Beorma Care*, a social enterprise dedicated to supporting home-based writers and artists who struggle with care and responsibility issues.

PAULINE E. DUNGATE came to Birmingham as a student at Aston University where she discovered the Aston SF Group and conventions. After graduating with a BSc in Geology and Chemistry she reluctantly took up teaching and after a number of years in Secondary Schools becam the resident teacher at the Science Museum. She writes short stories and poetry (often set in and about Birmingham) and is putting the finishing touches to a novel set in the city.

JULIUS HORNE was a white witch born in Birmingham on Halloween in 1906. Grateful to have avoided living in a time when the laws of *peine forte et dure* were being implemented, Julius spent the years before WWII working as a retail manager in Birmingham city centre whilst surreptitiously studying the occult. What happened between 1940 and 1966 remains shrouded in mystery, but upon retirement Julius finally began putting pen to paper. Now, in the twenty-first century, these works are finally able to see print.

ADRIAN MIDDLETON was born a Staffie, in the town of Wednesbury to the west, but has lived and worked in Birmingham (or at the very least mere yards from its border) since the age of four, but declines to admit how many years that has been. His passion for the city and its history is perhaps reflected by his stubborn refusal to let 'them diwwun souf' have all the fun.

He is a publisher, editor of several books and author of countless short stories (countless because they were usually written for old 'zines under pseudonyms he has a tendency to forget).

ANNE NICHOLLS rose to literary prominence as Anne Gay, writing a number of science fiction and fantasy novels including *Mindsail, The Brooch of Azure Midnight* and *Dancing on the Volcano*. She has also been a teacher, self-help author, agony aunt and counsellor. Now best known as a broadcaster, she lives in Birmingham with her husband, the fantasy author Stan Nicholls.

MIKE WATTS is a Birmingham based Illustrator and Graphic Designer with a strong interest in history, fantasy and science fiction. Introduced to the genres by authors such as Edgar Rice Burroughs and Michael Moorcock, Jack Vance and *Dungeons and Dragons* role playing games. He worked for many years in advertising and design agencies both in and around the city before became freelance a few years ago. He is eager to combine his interests with a pride in Brum and its often forgotten folklore and to expand more into illustration.

See more of his work at www.bigbeano.co.uk.

AFTERWORD

This book has been an experiment. If, like me, you're passionate about Birmingham and its rich, if unexplored, history, then we will have succeeded if something—has kindled your desire either to take a walk through the city, learn a little more about its history or, most importantly, to write about either Birmingham or your local places. Storytelling is not just inspired by what is out there, but also by the imagination. If we have helped you to see and feel the things that aren't visible, then...job done.

ADRIAN MIDDLETON, SEPTEMBER 2013

BEORMA CARE
COMMUNITY INTEREST COMPANY

Supporting Writers and Artists

Based in Birmingham, Beorma Care is a new social enterprise providing support to home-based freelancers within the creative industries, particularly writers and artists.

While many of these people give up work to create, many seek to work in these industries *because* of their personal situations. Whatever those situations may be – caring responsibilities, disability issues, dealing with discrimination, jobseeking or even more complex needs such as addiction or mental health issues, they are in danger of becoming isolated, reluctant to share their experiences lest it damage their reputation, or struggling to compete in a competitive marketplace where employers bear no responsibility for dealing with their circumstances.

Our goal is to provide information, advice, advocacy and support to our clients in order to:

- demonstrate and raise awareness of the issues

- build a network capable of mutual support

- remove barriers

- improve quality of life and work experience

- increase the opportunities

The Digbeth Trust is a registered charity and membership organisation that has been supporting small voluntary and community organisations in Birmingham and the West Midlands since 1986.

We provide development support and funding for grass roots organisations and social enterprises and bring together VCS organisations under consortia arrangements to bid for and deliver public service contracts. With a successful track record of reaching marginalised communities, we undertake community consultation and research projects through Community Pathways CIC and are experienced managers of grant programmes for public sector and charitable funders.

Enterprise Catalyst 2 Programme

The Digbeth Trust, in partnership with Enterprising Communities, Business and Learning, Business Insight and Winning Moves, is assisting in the delivery of the Enterprise Catalyst 2 programme, funded by the European Regional Development Fund (ERDF).

The Digbeth Trust is engaging with individuals to help develop their ideas for social enterprise and supporting them to access the funding process to turn this idea into a reality.

WHAT IS IT?

- Help for an individual to move from an "enterprise idea" to something more tangible
- Assistance for a business at its inception stage
- support for business survival
- support for business development

WHO IS IT FOR?
Individuals living in, or established registered businesses in, any of the following wards in Birmingham:

Aston, Bordesley Green, Hodge Hill, Ladywood, Lozells and East Handsworth, Moseley and Kings Heath, Nechells, Soho, South Yardley, Sparkbrook and Washwood Heath.

WHAT DOES DIGBETH TRUST OFFER?

- Pre-start and start up support for Social Enterprises, which includes: Analysis of your social enterprise idea;
- Initial support needs analysis;
- Help with legal structures and governance;
- Help to identify fundraising opportunities;
- Mentoring support;
- Access to specialist workshops;
- Access to networking opportunities;
- Action planning;
- Help to develop and hone your "pitch"
- Access to a "Dragons Den" type enterprise generator for a kick start grant of £250;
- Help to apply for the Enterprise Catalyst Acorn Fund grant of up to £1000.

 EUROPEAN UNION
Investing in Your Future
European Regional
Development Fund 2007-13

 ENTERPRISE™
CATALYST
AN ENTERPRISING
COMMUNITIES BUSINESS
SUPPORT INITIATIVE

Printed in Great Britain
by Amazon.co.uk, Ltd.,
Marston Gate.